P9-DUH-457

Emma

sugar and
spice and
everything
nice

If you purchased this book without a cover, you should be aware that this book is stolen property. It was reported as "unsold and destroyed" to the publisher, and neither the author nor the publisher has received any payment for this "stripped book."

This book is a work of fiction. Any references to historical events, real people, or real places are used fictitiously. Other names, characters, places, and events are products of the author's imagination, and any resemblance to actual events or places or persons, living or dead, is entirely coincidental.

SIMON SPOTLIGHT

An imprint of Simon & Schuster Children's Publishing Division

1230 Avenue of the Americas, New York, New York 10020

Copyright © 2013 by Simon & Schuster, Inc.

All rights reserved, including the right of reproduction in whole or in part in any form.

SIMON SPOTLIGHT and colophon are registered

trademarks of Simon & Schuster, Inc.

Text by Elizabeth Doyle Carey

Chapter header illustrations by Emmy Reis

Designed by Laura Roode

For information about special discounts for bulk purchases, please contact

Simon & Schuster Special Sales

at 1-866-506-1949 or business@simonandschuster.com.

Manufactured in the United States of America 0516 OFF

First Edition 4 6 8 10 9 7 5 3

ISBN 978-1-4424-7481-9 (pbk)

ISBN 978-1-4424-7488-8 (hc)

ISBN 978-1-4424-7489-5 (eBook)

Library of Congress Catalog Card Number 2013939387

CUPCAKE DIARIES

WITHDRAWN

Emma
sugar and spice and everything nice

by coco simon

Simon Spotlight

New York   London   Toronto   Sydney   New Delhi

CHAPTER I

Poor Jake

"Please, Emmy! Just one more lick!"

My younger brother, Jake, was whining at me, which always drives me crazy. I sighed in exasperation.

"Come on, Em, don't be such a tough guy," said my best friend Alexis. Though Jake's the only person I've allowed to call me "Emmy," lately everyone's been calling me "Em," though my full first name is "Emma."

"Great, now you're on his side?" I complained.

"I'm always on his side," said Alexis, winking at my little brother.

The Cupcake Club—my best friends Alexis, Mia, and Katie, plus me—were having a baking session in my kitchen. Whenever we bake at my house, my little brother, Jake, always comes scrounging around for tastes and licks of the batter and frosting, and he's so high maintenance that it drives me crazy.

Jake smiled up at me now with his most winning grin. Alexis put her arm across his shoulders.

"Come on, Em," she said.

"Fine, but he's eating up our profits, you know," I said, trying to appeal to Alexis's astute business sensibility. "Here, at least use a clean spoon. You've had a sore throat."

"I always have a sore throat!" cried Jake, gleefully scooping a big lump of buttercream frosting out of the mixing bowl.

"Strep again?" asked Mia, her brow wrinkling in concern.

I sighed. "Probably."

Jake was right; he *does* always have a sore throat. And usually an ear infection to go with it. The doctor says Jake's just prone to infections, because of the way his throat and ear canals are built. I can't think about things like ear canals too much because I get really queasy with body stuff, especially if it comes down to words like pus, or needles, or most especially, blood (even the word, never mind the sight of it!). Lately, I've even started to faint at the doctor's office and twice, almost, at the dentist's.

Most people don't know this about me, because I'm pretty embarrassed about it. It just seems weak and a little babyish, especially at my age. Alexis was at the doctor's office with me once when I had to get a shot and a blood test, so she knows all about it, but no one else really does.

Anyway, I do feel bad for Jake, with all the ear and throat problems, but I am a tiny bit jealous sometimes that he gets to stay home from school so much. Mom makes him soup and pudding, and he watches cartoons in his cozy clothes all day. It looks like heaven, and a sore throat seems like a small price to pay.

Just then my older brother Matt walked in, calling out a hello as he dumped his backpack in his locker in the mudroom. (Yes, we have lockers at home. Kind of pathetic, but my mom says it's the only way to contain the chaos with four busy and athletic kids in the house.) Matt's only a grade ahead of me, so we see each other a lot at school as well as at home, obviously, but Jake doesn't see him that much, so he gets bowled over by excitement when Matt shows up.

"Matty! Come see my drawing I did of the Miami Heat!" says Jake, dropping his spoon with a clatter into the sink and taking off.

"Hey! What about us?" asked Mia, who is Jake's special buddy.

But he didn't even hear her.

"The second you arrive, we're dead to him," joked Alexis, who has a crush on Matt. *The same can be said about you, my friend,* I thought, suppressing a giggle.

Matt smiled and shrugged, palms up in the air. "Hey, I can't help it if the kid worships me. Either you've got it or you don't got it, you know?"

"Trust me, you *don't* got it," I said, turning to the sink to start the cleanup.

Jake came tearing back in, a piece of drawing paper flapping in his hands. "Look! Look, Matty, isn't it cool? See that's LeBron, and that's Ray Allen, and here's the basket, and here's you and me in the stands. . . ."

Matt glanced down at it. "Sweet," he said, barely standing still for even a second. He passed by Jake, went to get a glass from the cabinet, and poured himself some juice. Jake stood still in the middle of the kitchen, unsure of whether to follow Matt or not.

"Hey, can I see it, Jake?" asked Katie, swooping in to mask Matt's lack of enthusiasm. She reached for the drawing, but Jake snatched it away.

"No! It's just for boys! It's basketball!" said Jake, all snotty.

"Jake! That's rude!" I cried. "Katie's just trying to—" I caught myself before I said "make you feel better." Phew. "Um, see how far your drawing's come," I finished lamely.

"No," said Jake. "Matty, what are you doing now?"

There was a pause as Matt finished gulping down his juice. "Homework," he said, clearing his throat and giving a huge burp.

All the girls groaned, but Jake giggled gleefully. "Good one!" Jake said.

"OMG, he even worships your burps," I said. "Pathetic."

Matt smiled and shrugged again. Then he reached out and tousled Jake's hair. "See ya later, little buddy." And he grabbed his backpack from the mudroom and then went upstairs.

Jake sat down in a kitchen chair, his drawing hanging limply from his side. He put his forehead in his hand, like he always does when he's thinking really hard.

"Want to draw with me?" asked Mia, who's very artistic. Jake loves drawing with her. She's so good, she can copy anything on paper and have it look like what it's supposed to, unlike me. Everything I draw ends up looking like a chicken.

Jake shook his head.

"What are you thinking about?" asked Katie, all perky and trying to cheer up Jake.

He looked at her and then kind of snapped out of his trance. "How I can draw better so Matty will like it."

We all looked at one another in pain. The poor kid. He so looks up to Matt and our oldest brother, Sam, but they are just too busy for him. I'm the one who spends all the time with him, but he couldn't care less about me, unless I have some sugary thing he wants to eat.

"Jake, you're a great artist!" Mia declared.

"Not that much," said Jake. He put his drawing on the kitchen table. "I'm going to watch TV," he said, and left the room.

"Okay, my heart is officially broken," said Mia once he was out of earshot.

"I know. It's sad," I agreed. "But he *is* high maintenance, and after a while it gets old."

"It would never get old for me," said Katie, who's an only child.

"Me neither," agreed Mia, who has only her older stepbrother, Dan.

I sighed heavily and sat down at the table, drying my hands on a dishtowel.

"I get it," said Alexis. "I still think it's sad, but I do get how Emma feels."

I alternated between feeling very sympathetic to Jake or very frustrated with him, sometimes within seconds. Like now.

"Okay, enough about Jake," I said. "Let's talk about what jobs we have lined up for the Cupcake Club."

We all sat at the table, and Alexis, who is our CEO, took out her laptop and began our meeting.

"Let's see, we have Mallory Clifford's birthday party this weekend. Three dozen Mud Pies. Plus Mona tomorrow . . ."

Mona is one of our regular customers. She owns The Special Day bridal salon and has a standing order for four dozen all-white mini cupcakes each Saturday. They're for her brides to eat, so they don't get all hungry and cranky while they're trying on dresses.

"Any modeling jobs coming up for you?" asked Katie.

I shook my head. I've done a bunch of modeling this year for Mona—mostly trunk shows, where I walk around in sample junior bridesmaids' dresses—but also a little bit of print work, which is really just another word for a newspaper or magazine ad. I got started doing a print ad for Mona, and other clients saw it. "There's not much on this month. It's kind of the off-season for trunk shows," I said. Even though I was kind of happy for the break (modeling is hard work, believe it or not), I could use some money. A little job would be okay right about now, especially some print work. The cash is good.

"Focus, people, and we can wrap this up," said Alexis, who is all about being an efficient manager.

"Oh, one of my mom's friends from work wants us to do a dessert for the book club she's hosting. My mom is going to it, too," said Mia. "I'll follow up on that." She punched a reminder into her phone.

"Good," said Alexis. "We could use some more business and some new clients. We need to branch out."

"Hey, don't forget we have that bachelorette party for Mona's client in two Saturdays," I said.

"Yup. Got it right here," said Alexis, looking at her calendar. "Three dozen. Our choice of flavor."

While we were reviewing the order, my mom walked in. "Hello, Cupcakers!" she greeted us

8

cheerily. My mom loves my friends, which gives me such a happy and cozy feeling.

"Hi, Mrs. Taylor!" they all replied. They love her too.

"What's up?" asked Alexis. My mom doesn't usually get home from work until five fifteen, and it was only four thirty now.

My mom grimaced. "I'm only here for a second. I have to take Jake to the doctor again. *They're talking about taking out his tonsils.*" She whispered the last part.

"Bummer," said Alexis.

"Dan had that done. It really hurts," whispered Mia.

"I know. But it's a pretty routine outpatient operation, and I guess the long-term payoff is worth it," said my mom.

"Definitely," Mia agreed, nodding. "He hasn't had a sore throat since."

"Well, here goes," said my mom. Then she called out, "Jake! Hi, honey! Time for the doctor!" and left the room in search of my little brother.

"I didn't want to say anything in front of your mom to worry her, but," said Mia quietly, "Dan couldn't eat anything but soft food for almost two weeks."

"Wow. Maybe we'll have to make Jake big bowls of frosting to fatten him up!" said Alexis.

"You're making me frosting?" asked Jake, walking into the room and shrugging on his hoodie at the same time.

"Maybe!" said Alexis, with a twinkle in her eye.

"I'll be good! I promise!" said Jake.

Mia grabbed him in a playful hug. "You're always good! It has nothing to do with that!" she said, tickling him.

He laughed and shrieked, and she let him go.

"Bye, big guy!" called Mia.

He waved and followed my mom out the door.

"He doesn't even know what's coming," said Katie mournfully.

"It's just tonsils!" I said, swatting her with the dishtowel. "He's not having heart surgery!"

But I knew Jake would not be psyched. It might as well be heart surgery. And deep down inside, I worried for him just the same.

CHAPTER 2

Good Guys Versus Bad Guys

The howling that night was unbearable. The doctor had decided Jake needed his tonsils out ASAP, and unfortunately he told Jake this directly. My mom said she would have preferred to ease Jake into the idea, but the doctor thought it better to be matter-of-fact and get it over with. Thus, the tantrum.

I was in my room with my fan turned way up to drown out Jake's wails. I tried practicing my flute, but it clashed so much with Jake's screams in the background that I finally gave up and just put my pillow over my head. By the time my mom called us all for dinner, I was worn out. I couldn't imagine how she was feeling.

It wasn't that I didn't understand how Jake was feeling, either. I mean, I'm terrified of needles and doctors and stuff; even the eye doctor! The idea of going to a hospital to get an operation is terrifying to me. So I kind of didn't blame him for making such a fuss.

At the dinner table, my mom and dad were tense; Matt was annoyed; and Sam was clueless, since he'd just arrived home from practice. Jake was taking a break from the wailing to give us all the silent treatment, and he sat at the table with his arms folded, his lips clamped shut against dinner, and his red-rimmed eyes downcast. I just wanted to shovel down my chicken fajita and then get the heck out of there.

"Emma, honey, there's a message on the machine for you," said my mom.

"From who?" I asked.

"Whom," corrected my mom, the librarian.

"From *whom*?" I repeated. I decided not to give her attitude right now, because I knew she'd snap.

She finished chewing her bite and then said, "It's from Alana Swenson's office. It's about a modeling job. They're doing some promotions for the hospital and want to know if you'd be interested in a photo shoot." (Alana became my agent after one of my first modeling jobs.)

"Isn't *that* ironic?" said Matt dryly.

12

My father shot him a warning look. We were not talking about Jake's operation at dinner.

"Okay. I might be interested, I guess." I shrugged, as if it was no big deal, but inside I felt weak and nervous just thinking about it. Modeling could be a little stressful, with everyone looking at you and poking and prodding you. However, the cupcake business had been slow lately, and I hadn't had much work from Mona, and I'd spent a bunch of money on some new attachments for my KitchenAid stand mixer and my frosting piper. I could really stand to make some cash.

"I'll call back in the morning and get the details, and then you can decide, okay?" asked my mom.

"Thanks."

We all ate in silence. Then Jake wondered, "Is that the same hospital?"

My mom and dad looked at each other, unsure what to say. Then my mom took a deep breath and said brightly, "Yes, honey. They want Emma to do some work for them. They're very nice over there."

I glanced at her, then I said, "Yeah, I could go check out that place for you. See what it's like. . . . Make some friends?" I looked at my mom again, and she was nodding encouragingly.

Jake was listening. He reached for his fajita,

13

hunger winning out over anger for the moment, so I kept talking. "It's pretty cool over there, from what I've heard. They have a really good gift shop, with toys and video games and stuffed animals. And there are some police officers there. . . ."

Jake's obsessed with law enforcement, so I decided to throw that in. He perked up.

"Why?" he asked through a mouth full of chicken and salsa.

"Um . . ." This one I wasn't sure how to handle, so I looked to my parents. Jake could smell a bad lie from a mile away, and it would set him off if he thought we were tricking him.

My parents gave each other a *What now?* look.

"To keep away the bad guys," said Sam.

Jake looked at him. "Why would there be bad guys?"

Uh-oh.

"Because the hospital is all good guys. And you know how bad guys like to fight good guys and take their stuff?"

Jake nodded.

"The cops keep the bad guys away," said Sam.

"Oh. That's cool," said Jake.

The rest of us breathed a sigh of relief, and my mom beamed at Sam.

14

"They also have really good ice cream, I've heard," said Matt, not to be outdone by Sam.

Jake scowled. "That's what the doctor said."

"Well, it's true," said Matt. "And they give you as much as you want. Popsicles, too."

"Really?" asked Jake cautiously.

"Uh-huh," Matt confirmed.

"I bet you could also have frosting if you wanted, right, Mom?" I added.

"I'll have to check, but I don't see why not," agreed my mom, almost giddy in her relief.

Jake looked down at his fajita and then shoved the last bite into his mouth. He mumbled something through the mouthful.

"What, sweetheart?" my mom asked cheerfully.

Jake finished chewing and then swallowed hard; it clearly hurt. We were all looking at him in anticipation.

"I'm still not going," he declared. And then he stood up from the table and left the room.

My parents looked deflated.

"When is the appointment supposed to be?" Sam asked quietly.

"The Friday after next," my mom said.

"So we have two weeks to work him up to it," Sam said.

"It almost would have been better if they were doing it immediately," Matt said.

"I agree," my dad said.

"Well, you'll just have to use a lot of bribery," I suggested.

"Great. Spoil him even more," Matt retorted.

"Matthew," my dad said in his warning voice.

"I'm just saying," Matt said with a shrug.

"It's going to be a tough two weeks," my mom said with a sigh.

The next morning my mom took me to the mall to make the cupcake delivery to The Special Day. While she went to Starbucks and then the bookstore, which both opened early, I trotted happily through the quiet shopping center, my cupcake carriers in hand. Jake had been zoned out in front of *SpongeBob* on TV when I left, but I gave him a little pat on the head that he didn't acknowledge.

In The Special Day, my friend Patricia, the manager, came to greet me at the door.

"Thank you, darling Emma!" she said with a warm smile. "Come, I'll get your money."

The Special Day is all white, sparkling clean, cool, and gently scented with something Patricia told me was linden blossom. It smells like a pretty garden. There are plump sofas, cushiony white rugs that absorb any noise, and classical music playing gently in the background. It is so peaceful, especially for people who live in boyland like me. I inhaled deeply and smiled. It was so nice to be away from all the boys at home, even for a tiny bit.

Patricia returned with the envelope of cash for me, and though I wanted to linger, I could tell she was busy and needed to get back to work.

"Another trunk show next month!" said Patricia. "We'll be in touch with the details!"

"Can't wait!" I said. "Bye!"

"See you soon, sweetie," she said as she closed the door behind me.

Outside, I felt kind of aimless. I folded the envelope, jammed it into the back pocket of my jeans, and strolled to the bookstore to find my mom.

"Hi, Mom," I said, plopping down next to her.

"Hey there, sweet pea," she said, absentmindedly reaching out and patting me on the back. She was engrossed in the paperback she'd picked out.

I looked around at the shelves to see if there was anything that might appeal to me, but it was all gory thrillers, and I am so not into that. The blood, remember?

I stood up. "Mom, I'm going to the YA section

to pick out a book. Come find me when you're ready to go."

"Mmm-hmm," she said.

I smiled and shook my head and then went to find something more to my taste.

It didn't take long before I too was curled up in a corner reading deeply and totally oblivious to the world around me. People came and went, and I didn't even look up.

Until I head my name.

"Emma!" a girl squealed.

I looked up.

Ugh.

It was Olivia Allen, our class's resident mean girl. Or mean-nice-mean girl, depending on the day, if you catch my drift. Olivia was as unpredictable as a roll of the dice. One day she'd be your best friend (usually if you had something she wanted), and then for a week she'd torture you. I generally avoided her to minimize the exposure.

"Hey, Olivia," I said, nice but not warm and friendly.

She was with an older girl. "Emma, this is my cousin Samantha, who's visiting from North Carolina. Sam, this is my friend Emma, who I model with."

I stood up; my parents have drilled good manners into me. "Nice to meet you," I said, smiling but feeling sorry for anyone related to Olivia Allen.

Olivia linked her arm through mine. "Emma and I are taking the city by storm!" she said to Samantha, and she laughed and tossed her hair.

It was true that Olivia and I had gone on a couple of the same go-sees for jobs, but we'd never actually modeled together. (A "go-see," in case you haven't guessed, is when you go see someone creating a commercial or ad, and then they decide if they want to use you as their model.) In fact, Olivia hadn't done any modeling jobs that I knew about. I smiled vaguely.

"Any good jobs coming up?" asked Olivia.

"Oh no. Nothing really," I said, crossing my toes at the lie. I wasn't about to tell her about the hospital call. Even if I didn't know if I wanted the job for myself, I certainly didn't want her to get it. Mostly because I couldn't stand the bragathon that would follow for months to come. "You?" I asked casually, not expecting anything.

"Actually, yes." She tossed her hair again. "I've got a booking with the hospital. They're doing some promotional work and selected me for the young person in the photos."

What?

So I said, "Oh, they already chose you? Because they called me yesterday and asked me to come down next week. So maybe I should just assume . . ."

Olivia's face reddened, and her cousin looked at her. "Oh, actually, I mean, well . . . they selected me to come in for a tryout next week. So . . . that's what I meant."

"So it's a go-see?" I prompted. I couldn't resist making her squirm.

"Yeah," she admitted quietly.

I fought a smile. "So maybe I'll see you there?" I asked.

"Totally!" Olivia brightened. "We could even go together if you want. My mom is taking me. . . ."

I thought back to my one and only, very unpleasant go-see with Olivia and her mom, when her mom yelled at her the whole way home for not getting the job. I couldn't go through that again!

"Oh no, thanks. My mom will take me," I said hurriedly. "She has some stuff to do down there, so . . ."

"Okay! Bye!" said Olivia quickly. And they left. She clearly didn't want to be caught out in any more lies.

I sat back down, but instead of starting my book

again, I bit my lip and replayed the conversation in my mind. I never like to be mean to people. But something about Olivia makes me just want to at least stick up for myself.

"Emma?" It was my mom.

"Over here," I whispered loudly, standing up again.

"Ready, honey?" she asked, smiling as she came into view.

"Ready!" I said. I squatted to reshelf the book, and we left. (Librarians and their families never buy books at bookstores!) We shopped a little before we got back in the car, stopping to check out Icon, this really cool store with trendy teen clothes. I had no money, and my mom didn't want to buy me the shirt I wanted, so we left. Shopping while broke is no fun.

It wasn't until I got home that I realized the envelope of Cupcake Club cash had fallen out of my pocket. It must've been all that standing up and sitting down! When my dad drove me back to retrace my steps, the envelope was nowhere to be found. And that meant I owed the Cupcake Club forty dollars that I didn't have. I e-mailed Alexis to let her know, and I promised to make it up to the club as soon as humanly possible, even though I was broke. She replied that she knew I was "good for it" and that I could have a couple of weeks to pay it back.

This meant I really needed some more work. I hate owing anyone money, especially my friends. I hoped the hospital modeling job would be mine!

CHAPTER 3

The Queasy Life

Even though I dreaded anything medical, I couldn't wait until Monday when my mom would get more info on the modeling job at the hospital. I was nervous that Olivia already had a leg up on me, and I needed the money. I wondered what the shoot would entail. Like, maybe it wasn't happening *at* the hospital, just because it was *for* the hospital. Or maybe it wouldn't be medical in nature at all! Maybe it would be, like, a happy, healthy family skipping down the street together . . . something to entice people before they stuck needles in them (kidding!).

Actually, because of my own medical fears, I could relate to Jake's fears about the hospital and the operation. I did honestly feel bad for the kid. At first. But after his horrible behavior all weekend—behavior that my mother excused as "nerves"—I was ready to lose my mind.

First of all, we went out for dinner on Saturday night for my dad's birthday, and Jake refused to order anything but ice cream. Specifically, the Oreo cookie sundae.

My dad tried to be firm at first, though my mom was ready to cave from the outset. The waitress took everyone's order but Jake's, and then she doubled back to see if he'd decided yet, and that's when things started to boil over. My dad said, "Just bring us some plain noodles with butter, please," and Jake started to wail. Then my dad was trying to shush him, and my mom put Jake on her lap, then my mom and dad began to fight about my mom babying Jake. People were looking at us from the neighboring tables, and Matt and Sam and I were just rolling our eyes and wishing we were *anywhere* else but there right then.

My mom was trying to reason with Jake, and Jake kept protesting that if he could eat ice cream all the time *after* his surgery, then why couldn't he start now? My father decided to ignore the two of them, and he and Matt and Sam went to the bar to catch the start of the baseball game on the TV there. That left me with my mom and the screaming creature also known as my baby brother. In the end, my mom had the waitress bring the Oreo sundae at the same time as the pasta, and Jake was supposed to eat the noodles while looking at the sundae, but you can imagine how long that lasted. In short, my poor dad's birthday dinner was a bust.

The next day, Jake and I went to the grocery store with my mom. I was superhelpful and ran around with half the list while also shopping for some Cupcake Club supplies with a list Alexis had given me. Meanwhile, Bratty Bratterson (my new name for Jake) was pulling every possible ice-cream flavor (Rocky road! Red velvet cake!) out of the freezer and piling them into my mom's cart. The only off-list thing I selected was this really good, *slightly* sugary cereal I'd had at Mia's one time on a sleepover, and when we got to the check-out, my mom said, "Emma, I don't *think* so! Unless you have your own money for this junk?" I obviously didn't, so she set it aside.

Meanwhile, when the checkout lady started to ring through Jake's ice-cream selections, my mother tried to ditch a couple of things, and Jake began to pitch a fit. My mom tried to reason with him, that the plainer the ice cream, the better it would feel sliding down after the operation, but he didn't want to listen. She insisted on at least one carton of vanilla and then sighed heavily and also let him get everything he wanted, explaining to me that it was just Jake's "nerves" that were making him behave so badly. *Right*.

The final straw was on Sunday afternoon, when my mom came back from Matt's game and had a small bag of presents for Jake—a team hat, a hoodie, and a mini basketball net and ball for his room.

"What does he get all this for?" I asked.

"Oh, Emma, you're really starting to become a counter," said my mother impatiently. Being a "counter" is a major insult in my family. It's what my parents say about people who are overly concerned about what others have and count all the things they want. As soon as she said it, I turned on my heel, went to my room, and firmly shut the door. (I didn't slam it, even though I really wanted to!) My mom came up later to apologize, but I didn't feel any better and I let her know it.

"You can't turn this whole family into Jake's slaves, just because you feel sorry for him!" I said.

"I know," my mother agreed, wearily rubbing her temples. "I just hate to see him so upset."

"He's upset because he's spoiled," I said.

"I guess he is," she replied.

I was momentarily thrilled that I'd gotten her to agree with a criticism of one of my brothers; usually, she just defends them or explains away their bad behaviors.

But then I felt guilty.

"All I'm saying is, the same rules should apply, even if he does have to go get a little operation," I persisted. "I bet part of why he's so upset is because you're being so overly nice to him; it's making him suspicious. So no matter what you say, all the presents and ice cream make him think the operation really *is* a big deal."

"I'm sure you're right," she agreed with me, sighing.

Great, and . . . ?

"I just feel bad for him," she said.

Aaargh!

I was relieved when the weekend was over and I got to leave my house and get away from the monster. I was actually looking forward to school. However, on Monday, all the Cupcakers wanted to know about was how "poor Jake" was, and "What can we do for him?" There was no escape!

At lunch, Mia, Katie, and Alexis brainstormed

27

about ways they could make him feel better, and in the end they decided that a little cupcake send-off next Thursday after school would be a great idea. Then they all begged to come to my house again after school today, to do some sample baking and taste testing with Jake, one of their favorite pastimes. (Since he is such a sugar nut, he's very gratifying to feed.) But I absolutely refused, insisting I needed to be away from that kid as much as possible or I would be tempted to take his tonsils out myself with my bare hands.

So after school the four of us trooped over to Katie's and had a little baking session there. (Katie: "I bet he'd love snickerdoodle, right, Emma?" Me: "What*ever*.") It *wasn't* the most fun I've ever had.

After about an hour the phone rang, and it was actually my mom calling for me.

"Hi, Mom," I said, taking the phone from Katie.

"Hi, honey, I spoke to the PR person at the hospital who's coordinating the shoot. She gave me the details, and she's going to have to know right away if you're interested, which is why I'm calling you."

"Great! What is it?"

There was a little pause. "Well, it's next Wednesday. . . . I know you usually only model on weekends, but just this once I'll make an exception."

"And?"

"Pretty good money: Three hundred dollars . . . for about two hours' work."

"And?" I was getting impatient. I could tell she was hiding something from me.

"Well, Em, it's for the blood drive, you know. It's a new campaign; they need more people to donate blood, so they're really going to play up the sympathy aspect. So they want to show a kid receiving blood, but they don't want to use a real sick kid, because that's too sad and may be too taxing for the child. So . . . it would mean sitting in a chair . . . in a hospital gown . . . with a bag of blood that looks like it's going into your arm. I'm sure it will be fake blood, though." My mom spoke quickly at the end.

Oh no.

"Um. Wow," I said.

I felt faint just thinking about it. I sat down on a stool at the kitchen counter.

"I know," my mom said quietly. Obviously, she knows how I am about all this stuff. "Do you want to think about it? Or should I just call back and say 'no, thanks'?"

I thought for a minute. First of all, I needed the

money. Second of all, I really didn't want Olivia Allen to get the job. Third of all, maybe I'd set a good example for Jake.

I sighed. "I'll do it," I said. "I'll try out."

"Are you sure, sweetheart?"

I took a deep breath. "Yes. Thanks."

We hung up, and I sat at the counter for another minute, trying not to think about a bag of blood—real or not—dripping into my arm.

"Hey, are you okay, Em?" asked Katie. She came over and put her hand on my arm. "You look pretty pale."

I smiled wanly. "I'm trying out for a modeling job, but . . ." I was embarrassed to admit my weakness; after all, only Alexis really knew about my superqueasiness.

Katie looked at me in concern. "But what?"

I took a deep breath. Might as well fess up. "It's for the hospital. For a blood drive. And I'm superqueasy. I kind of faint at the mention of blood, never mind the sight of it."

Mia looked up. "You kook! Don't do the shoot, then! Just say no!"

"But I need the money," I said.

Alexis stood and came to my side. "If this is about the money you lost, don't worry about it. You can

30

have an extension. I don't want you fainting just to get money for us," she said.

"Thanks." I sighed. "I guess part of it is that . . . well, I just hate to be weak, you know? And let my fears rule my life. Like, I should be able to do this! I mean, I'm not Jake! I'm tough!"

"You go, girl!" said Mia.

"Well, you know they won't actually put the needle in you for the photo shoot, right?" asked Katie.

"No, I know. It's just the idea of it. And being in the hospital. And do you think they'll use real blood?"

"No way!" said Mia.

"I just . . . I mean, I can't even deal with shots. Like, not even Novocain at the dentist." I grimaced.

"A shot is only a couple of seconds, Em," said Alexis kindly. "Remember when I went with you? You thought they still hadn't done it, and it was over."

"I know. I guess I just work myself up," I said.

"Want us to have a cupcake party for you, too, after the shoot?" asked Alexis with a grin.

But Katie was thinking. "You know," she said after a pause. "My mom is known for being really great with people who are really nervous about going to the dentist. Do you want me to see if she'd give you some advice or whatever? Tips on how to cope? Then you could use them at the shoot, but also maybe in real life?"

I couldn't imagine it would help, but it was nice of Katie to offer, so I had to say yes. "Thanks. Sure. That would be great."

Katie nodded her head briskly. "Good. Let's do it this weekend. You can come over on Saturday afternoon, after my mom's morning office hours, and she'll work on you."

Work on me?

I gulped. "Okay."

"Okay, back to cupcakes," said Alexis, ever the boss. "Let's review our agenda." She took out her notebook. "First, we have Mona this Friday. We have Jake's party next Thursday. We have Mona to bake for next Friday and also her client with the bachelorette party. What are we making for that?" She chewed on the end of her pen.

"Are we doing something wild or traditional?" asked Mia, her creative juices already flowing.

"Wild," said Alexis, consulting her notes. Alexis had recently created a brilliant worksheet that we now used with all our clients. It had an outline of a cupcake in the middle, then headings listed in the margins, with lists of choices below them: "Cake Flavor," "Frosting Flavor," "Toppings," "Decor," "Inspiration," and "Please Avoid." At the bottom were some empty lines for writing notes.

"Flavor choices?" asked Katie, closing her eyes to focus.

Alexis looked down. "Cake flavor: The bride-to-be said we could pick the flavor! Avoid: nuts, fruit. Sparing use of chocolate, if any. Toppings and decor are up to us. For inspiration, the bride loves lace and vampires."

"Should we work in some bacon?" I suggested. Bacon caramel cupcakes are my trademark; I invented them, and they've been wildly popular with our clients.

"Maybe a little too ... manly ... for a bachelorette party," said Mia tactfully.

True. I nodded.

"Let's do something vampirish," said Katie. "Like you'd make for Bella from the Twilight books."

"Ooh, spooky!" said Alexis. "Like what?"

"Red velvet?" I suggested.

"Or what about . . . You could do something with bright-red cream in the middle, so it oozes out when you bite into it," Mia said, her eyes twinkling mischievously.

"Yes!" I agreed.

"The outside could be all white. White cake, white smooth frosting . . . ," said Katie, "so no one suspects what's inside!"

"We could lay them out on lacey doilies," I added.

Alexis typed furiously on her laptop to keep up with our ideas.

Mia clapped her hands gleefully. "I love it! Pure-white, innocent, bridal-looking cupcakes on lace, and when you bite into them, all that red blood dripping down your chin!"

Ugh. "When you put it that way . . . ," I said, my stomach turning over suddenly.

"Oh, Em, don't worry. It will only be raspberry or cherry or something! Plus, you'll be much better after my mom's training session," said Katie, patting my arm and smiling.

"I sure hope so," I replied.

I couldn't be worse.

34

CHAPTER 4

The Four Ds

I suffered through the week of Jake's bad behavior and my parents' pathetic reactions to it, and then it was Saturday and time to go to Katie's for my "training." The others were going to be there too, because they wanted to bake some samples for Jake's big send-off for him to try later.

When I got to Katie's, Dr. Brown was ready and waiting, and she greeted me with a hug and a big smile. I was so nervous, I was shaking, even though, obviously, she wasn't going to do anything to me. I mean, I was pretty sure she wasn't going to give me a shot or anything. We were supposed to just talk in her study while the others worked in the kitchen. Or that's what she told my mom, who thought it was a great idea.

"I'll have a treat for you, after," promised Katie.

"Great," I said weakly, wiping my sweaty palms on my jeans. "Thanks."

I slowly walked down the carpeted back hall to Dr. Brown's study, and she told me to sit on the sofa and to just relax.

"So, Emma, I understand you're nervous around needles and blood," she began.

I nodded. "Anything medical, really. Or dental," I added. "Or the eye doctor."

Dr. Brown looked thoughtful. "Have you always felt this way, or is it a new fear?" she asked kindly.

I had to think about that for a minute. "Well, I've always been nervous about it, but it's gotten worse. And the fainting is new. It's like . . . I know what's coming, and I dread it, so it happens."

"You mean the fainting?" Dr. Brown prompted.

"Uh-huh."

"Have you ever been told you might have low blood pressure?" she asked.

"Well, the nurse always says 'very good' when she takes off the cuff."

Dr. Brown chuckled. "The reason I ask is that most people who faint do it because their blood pressure drops; if you have low blood pressure to begin with, it doesn't have far to drop before you're out! I'll ask your mom later, because there are special things you can do to combat it from that angle, like drinking a lot of fluids before you go."

"Okay," I said.

"But that's the physical part. Mentally, there are quite a few tools you can use to arm yourself against medical stress and fainting. I call the most important ones the 'three Ds': desensitize, deep breathing, and distraction."

I nodded.

"'Desensitize' means to get used to something, so you're not as sensitive to it. One way to do that is to expose you to the stressor—whatever makes you nervous—over and over again, until it becomes routine. For instance, I have some patients come and sit in the chair, and we do a mini cleaning for maybe five minutes, and that's it. Just so they can get used to the process, the setting, the instruments, the smells and sounds of everything. Once you get used to something, and it becomes familiar, it loses its novelty and your body doesn't react to it as strongly the next time. Does that make sense?"

"Yes," I replied. "It sounds like a lot of work, though."

Dr. Brown laughed. "It is, but you don't take a lot of time each session, and it pays off, big time. The next tactic, the deep breathing, is self-explanatory. Part of our reaction when we get nervous is to freeze up, to tighten our chest, and to take shallow breaths. This is actually the opposite of what your body needs when you are trying to calm down. What you need is to take slow, long, deep breaths. Let's try it. In through your nose, out through your mouth." She inhaled slowly and deeply through her nose, and I copied her. Then she let it out through her pursed lips, like she was blowing soap bubbles. We did it a few times, and though I was a little wobbly at first, my breathing did steady somewhat after a few tries.

"Good! You're a fast learner!" said Dr. Brown, clapping for me.

"Wow, I'm a great breather!" I joked. "There's a skill."

"Oh, but it is," Dr. Brown insisted. "If you can control your breathing, you can control your reaction to almost anything. That's what meditation is all about, actually. But, anyway, the third D is 'distraction.' You need to use everything you've got to keep your mind thinking about other stuff while you're being subjected to your stressors—needles or blood or what have you. So, an iPod, a book, chewing gum, a squeeze ball—anything that takes even part of your attention away from the situation is good."

"My dentist does that. They set up a movie for me to watch. But I still get stressed!" I said. "So I guess the distraction thing really doesn't work for me."

Dr. Brown bit her lip thoughtfully. "Well, there are a couple of possibilities. For one, you need to switch up the distractions, so that they really do distract you. Some things work better than others, and some you just get used to and they lose their novelty. Also, if you're starting to work yourself up as soon as you get to the doctor or dentist's office, you're almost coming in too late with the distractor. Your body is already in its fight-or-flight response. Your heart is beating fast, the adrenaline is coursing through your system, your senses are heightened, your sinuses are clear, and your reflexes are twitching and raring to go."

"Yup, that sounds like me in the waiting room!" I said, laughing darkly.

"So you need to sequence things right. Start with desensitizing. You can come to my office and practice some of that if you'd like. Next, distract. Then, deep breath. I promise you it all takes just a small effort, but the payoff is huge. And I'll share my very last tip with you. It's kind of a silly one, but it does work. Think of someone you admire—someone practical, no-nonsense, successful—and picture them in the same situation and how they'd handle it."

I thought for a minute, and besides my parents, I actually came up with Mona, from The Special Day. She is all of those things and more, and someone I admire. I tried to picture her in the dentist chair or getting her blood drawn and I had to smile.

Dr. Brown smiled back at me. "Good! I can see you've got someone!"

I nodded. "It's Mona from the bridal store. I have to giggle picturing her. In the store she's always saying things are 'divine,' so now I'm picturing her in the dentist's chair saying, 'Divine! Divine!'"

"'Divine' is good!" cried Dr. Brown, clapping her hands. "That should be your new motto. It makes you giggle, and it reminds you of someone you admire. I love it!"

I grinned. "Thanks for all this," I said.

"It is absolutely my pleasure," said Dr. Brown. "And you're smart to tackle this while you're young. I can't tell you how many adults I treat who've let their fears grow so large that it dominates them and compromises their health. They put off cleanings and checkups and dental work, all because they're nervous, and in the long run, they suffer. A healthy fear of danger is one thing, but nerves are another. If nerves rule your life, you'll miss out!"

It was true. Now I felt inspired, like I could fight any battle. I stood up. "Okay! I wish I was going to get a shot right now," I declared. "I'm all fired up!"

"Great!" said Dr. Brown with a smile. "Just remember the four *D*s: desensitize, deep breathing, distracting, and . . . ?"

"Divine!" I said, laughing.

We walked back to the kitchen, where everyone was happily working.

"How did it go?" asked Katie, her look of concern lightening when she saw that we were smiling.

"Very well!" said Dr. Brown. "Emma's a natural."

"Good," said Katie, relieved.

"I knew you'd tackle it!" called Mia from the other side of the kitchen.

"And, remember, I can fit you in any time for a five-minute cleaning. Maybe one day this week?" asked Dr. Brown.

"Thanks," I said. "I'll tell my mom to set it up."

"Okay, time for your prize, just like I promised!" singsonged Katie. She went to the pantry and came back with a cupcake on a plate. It was a yellow cupcake, and she had piped the words "Your Prize" on it. She handed it to me. "They're called Brave Butterscotch cupcakes. I originally invented them for Jake, but I think you've earned it instead!"

"Thanks, Katie. Yum!" I peeled the wrapper and began to eat it right there and then, suddenly ravenous after my session with Dr. Brown.

"Hey, what about me?" asked Dr. Brown.

"I have one for you too!" Katie went to get it.

We spent the rest of the afternoon in a kind of bake-off, with each of my friends trying to create something that Jake would love. It was semi-annoying to me. Only "semi" because I was touched that my friends cared so much about my little brother; "annoying" because he is.

Katie made everyone laugh when she said she wanted to bake Jake a special cupcake that was sugar and spice and everything nice, because that's what little boys are made of. But Mia pointed out that the rhyme says that's what little girls are made of, while boys are made of snips and snails and puppy dog's tails. Katie's face was priceless.

"What? No," she said, sure of herself.

But Mia shook her head, and Alexis and I backed her up, laughing our heads off.

"But we can't do snail cupcakes. It would ruin our reputation," said Alexis.

"Not to mention our baking equipment!" I said with a shudder.

But Katie said, "Oh whatever! I'm making him something sugary and spicy, anyway."

"Well, then, maybe it will help, because he's sure not nice!" I declared.

That evening Dr. Brown dropped the Cupcakers and me off at my house with a platter of samples for Jake, so he could choose which cupcake he liked best for his party. Alexis also had the platter of vampire samples, because she and her mom would be dropping them off on their way home later for the bachelorette's hostess to approve. Matt and Sam were both home, and they instantly began to hover once they discovered what we had for Jake. But Mia slapped their hands away and went to get Jake from the TV room.

Jake strolled in like a prince, and the girls eagerly began describing what they'd made, each one lobbying hard for her own idea, like we were in a bake-off or something.

"See, Jakey, these are Snickerdoodles," said Katie, pushing one toward him. "They have cinnamon, like cookies, and a cream cheese frosting. Sugar and spice and everything nice!" She smiled encouragingly.

"But these Monster cakes are the best ones, really," said Mia, edging her creations forward on the platter. "They're much bigger, and they're fudgy chocolate with chunks of chocolate inside them, and the frosted cupcakes are dunked in chocolate sprinkles!"

Jake's eyes widened.

"Try mine first, though!" said Alexis. "They're P-B-and-Js, with peanut butter frosting. The perfect kid's cupcake; no adults allowed!"

"Dude, you are one lucky little man," said Sam as he sat on a kitchen stool and surveyed all the offerings. "Anything you don't want, I'll have."

Across the counter, Jake spied the plate of vampire cupcakes. "What are those?" he asked, his eyes narrowing.

"Oh, these are samples for another client. A lady who's getting married," said Alexis dismissively.

Jake eyed them. "Are they just vanilla vanilla, like you make for Mona?" he asked.

Mia's eyes lit up. "Yes, but there's a big surprise inside! He can try one, can't he?" she asked, turning to the rest of us.

44

I sighed. "Of course he wants the ones that aren't for him," I said.

"Let me try one!" Jake whined, already starting to tune up a major show.

"Oh, here we go," said Matt, and he turned on his heel and then left the room.

"Fine by me," said Alexis with a shrug.

"Are you sure you don't want to try the Snickerdoodle?" asked Katie hopefully.

"Oh, give it a rest with the Snickerdoodle already!" said Mia, laughing. "If I even hear that word one more time . . ."

"Snickerdoodle, Snickerdoodle, Snickerdoodle!" chanted Katie with an evil grin.

Alexis selected a vampire cupcake for Jake and handed it to him.

"This I've got to see," said Sam, watching.

Jake picked up the cupcake and eyed it suspiciously. "I just bite it normal?" he asked.

"Yes, normal," instructed Mia. Her face was made all woozy by Jake's cuteness.

Barf.

"Here, hold this under your chin, though," said Alexis, offering Jake a paper towel.

Jake peeled the wrapper and took a bite. Instantly, the fake blood, which was really raspberry jam, burst from the inside and started to leak out the sides of the cupcake and drip onto the paper towel. We put in a lot, so wherever you bit the cupcake, it would spurt out.

"Oh, gnarly!" cried Sam, covering his face and turning away, laughing.

"Gross!" I said. I hadn't seen the full effect on an innocent taster yet. I breathed deeply and channeled Mona, trying to think of her reaction in the face of gore: *Divine! Just divine!* It kind of worked.

Meanwhile, Jake dropped the cake back onto the plate, and for a second I thought he was going to pitch a fit; he did not like to feel as if he was the butt of a joke or as if people were laughing at him. But his showmanship won out, and a smile crept over his face. "That's awesome!" he yelled. And he picked up the cupcake and then took another big bite, getting more "blood" on his face.

"What are you kids—Oh my goodness!" my mother yelled as she walked into the kitchen and saw Jake covered in "blood." She ran to his side. "Jake!" she shrieked, and at this point we all were laughing hysterically. Jake knew he'd pulled a fast one on our mom, and he was thrilled.

"I want these!" he declared, the raspberry filling staining his teeth. "These cupcakes rule!"

46

"But what about my yummy Snickerdoodles?" asked Katie quietly, with a fake sad face. She lifted it off the plate and then handed it to Sam with a shrug. "Here you go, I guess."

"Thanks. Snickerdoodle cupcakes rule!" he joked, echoing Jake. But Katie looked pleased, so it was all worth it.

Matt came back and gobbled up a P-B-and-J and two Monster cupcakes. Luckily, with three brothers selecting cupcakes, everyone won in the end.

CHAPTER 5

The Fifth D

$\mathcal{M}$y mom arranged for me to see Dr. Brown after school on Monday. We really didn't have any time to waste since the modeling go-see was on Wednesday.

I really dreaded the appointment all day, to be honest.

By the time my mom got home to pick me up at 3:45, I felt sick and shaky. Jake was coming with us, and he was starting to gloat a little, singsonging about how "Emmy's scared of the dentist!" I wanted to throttle the kid, but the anger *did* help distract me. (Note to self: have Jake annoy me before my modeling appointment on Wednesday.)

When we got to Dr. Brown's, it was kind of busy, since she'd wedged me in. There were two little kids in the waiting area, younger than Jake (he distanced himself from them immediately and began "reading" a magazine rather than play at the LEGOs table with them), and a really cute boy I recognized from school named Diego Diaz.

Of course I was totally fidgety and nervous and kept trying to read a magazine, chew gum, take deep breaths—all the things Dr. Brown had told me to do. Diego was just sitting there, doing nothing much except laughing at the cute little kids while they played. He was totally relaxed! That was a little intimidating; cute *and* relaxed. Hmph!

Dr. Brown's assistant called Diego in first, and he smiled at me as he stood to go in for his appointment. I kind of smiled back—it was more of a grimace—but I was pretty psyched he'd even acknowledged me. Inside the examining room, I could hear Dr. Brown greeting him and the two of them chatting and laughing. Laughing! At the dentist's office! Can you imagine?

I bit my nails and did my deep breathing, comforting myself that I had a while to go. But just a few minutes later, Dr. Brown's assistant called me in to the other examining room. I was shocked! I thought I'd have at least twenty more minutes before it was my turn. I stood on shaky legs as my mom whispered, "Do you want me to come with you?" I shook my head no. If I was ever going to be able to do this, I'd have to do it alone.

Inside the examining room, the assistant settled me on to the reclining chair, but once I was in it, she sat it upright, so it was more like a chair than a bed. She smiled. "My name's Nina. I know you're used to Joanne, but she has today off. Dr. Brown said you're a little nervous, so I always think it's a good idea to start out upright in the chair. Lying down makes you feel like things aren't in your control, and that can make you nervous, don't you think?"

Nina was pretty and chipper and young. She didn't seem nervous about anything! I nodded, not trusting my voice.

"Do you remember about the breathing?" she asked. "Long, slow breaths; in through your nose and out through your mouth." She did it a few times, and I copied her, watching her face for guidance. I did start to feel a little better. Nina smiled.

"Here's a squishy ball for distraction," she said, handing me a little rubber ball to squeeze. "And did you bring an iPod or anything?"

I waved my iPod at her.

"That's good!" she said. "Keep doing the deep

50

breathing!" She jokingly wagged her finger at me.

There was a little rap on the door, and Dr. Brown came bustling in. "Emma! Hello! I'm so glad you could make it," she said. She came over and gave me a hug. She smelled clean and comforting, and I almost didn't want to let go.

"Now, I have something a little different for you today, but I think it's going to be helpful." She nodded at Nina. "Emma's going to do a little observation first, just for a few minutes, okay?"

"Great!" said Nina.

"Emma, come with me," said Dr. Brown, so I climbed out of the chair and followed her.

Down the hall, we entered the room where Diego was waiting, lying in an examining chair that had been tipped all the way back. He smiled and gave a little wave!

"Oh, hi!" I said, feeling shy.

"Diego Diaz, this is Emma Taylor. Emma, this is Diego."

"Nice to meet you," I said.

"I recognize you from school," he said. "You're Matt's sister, right?"

"Yes, among others," I said, and rolled my eyes.

"Emma has three brothers," said Dr. Brown. "Isn't she lucky?"

I laughed. "I don't know if that's the right word for it!" I said.

"Sounds to me like you won the lottery!" teased Diego.

The laughing made me feel better. (It's amazing, the positive side effects of a cute guy making jokes!)

"Okay. So, Emma. Knowledge is power, right?" said Dr. Brown.

I nodded.

"Great, then we're going to let you see what we're doing during a cleaning, so you don't get nervous. Right, Diego?"

"Right," he confirmed.

"Sit right here, Emma," she said, pulling another swivel stool up next to Diego.

"Okay, sunglasses." Dr. Brown handed Diego a cool pair of shades, which he put on. "These are to block out the bright examining light a little," she said to me.

Diego gave me the thumbs-up.

"Now the bib," she said as she fastened a protective cloth around Diego's neck. "This keeps the toothpaste and stuff off your nice clean clothes."

I nodded again.

"Now the suction." She held up a bent tube and flipped a switch, showing me how weak its suction was on my hand. She switched to a clean tip and then put it in Diego's mouth. "To suck up the extra toothpaste," she explained.

I knew all this, so it wasn't exactly new information, but I was kind of interested to see Diego get his teeth cleaned. He had very nice teeth—white, even, strong. I had to remind myself why I was there a few times.

Then Dr. Brown got down to business. First, she showed me her tools, then she reminded me to breathe, because there might be a little blood. Then she numbed his gums with some gel and then started to clean.

I watched as she kind of scraped the edges of Diego's teeth. It amazed me that he held so still while she was doing it. I am a known squirmer at my usual dentist, and the hygienist often has to stop, so I can settle myself down. But Diego was peaceful, listening to his iPod, tapping his toe in sync with the beat coming through his headphones. Every once in a while Dr. Brown would say, "Okay, Diego?" and he'd nod.

It was weird actually seeing her perform what I had only pictured in my mind for years. What feels like violent scraping when it's your own mouth only looks like gentle wiping when it's someone else's mouth. But while she was working on a molar, she scraped some of his gum, and it suddenly started to bleed.

"Oh!" I said, turning away as the blood seeped into his mouth and was sucked away by the little tube. Instantly, my body started its usual reaction: noises got far away, drowned out by a rushing sound in my ears, my face grew warm, and my head felt weak. Nina stood beside me and held my shoulders.

Do not faint in front of a cute guy! I scolded myself. *Do* not *do it!*

"It's okay, just a very tiny bit of blood," said Dr. Brown. "Did that hurt, Diego?"

He shook his head no.

"You've got to do a little better on the flossing in the back. Otherwise, things are looking great, okay, honey?"

I couldn't believe she was so businesslike in the face of blood. And Diego was totally unfazed!

She glanced at me. "You all right?"

I took a deep breath, in through my nose, out through my mouth. Then I nodded. *Shape up, Emma!* I told myself. *You're just a bystander! This isn't even happening to you!* I steadied myself and took another very deep breath. *Divine! Divine!* I channeled Mona a little bit.

"It's mind over matter, Emma," she said. "And I know you are brave in many other ways, so just decide to add this to your list, okay?" She smiled at me.

I nodded in what I hoped was a firm, Mona-esque style. *Divine!*

Dr. Brown winked at me and whispered, "It's divine, right?"

I giggled in spite of myself.

After Dr. Brown finished the bottom row of his teeth, she suctioned Diego's mouth all over and tilted his chair up, so he could rinse and spit.

"How was it?" she asked him. He tipped up his sunglasses onto his head. "Fine," he said.

"Did it hurt?" she asked.

"Not really," he said. "It's just a little pinching, but it goes away fast. Nothing worse than what my sister does to me on a regular basis." Diego grinned.

"Okay, Emma?" asked Dr. Brown.

"Yeah. It wasn't as bad as I pictured," I said, crossing my fingers at the lie. "Thanks for letting me watch," I said to Diego. I still felt a little weak, but I wasn't as shaky as I usually would have been.

"Anytime," he said.

Dr. Brown left Nina in charge of finishing Diego, and she brought me back to my examining room. I got nervous again as I sat down, but she reminded me to breathe, and handed me a mirror so I could watch, and sunglasses to block the light, and she left me sitting pretty upright, so I would feel in control. I turned up the volume on my iPod and tried to picture Mona getting her teeth cleaned and how well she'd handle it. But my thoughts kept drifting back to Diego. He really was cute. I owed it to him to not pass out!

Dr. Brown washed her hands and did a mock cleaning, where she gelled my gums for numbness, then very gently did a tiny cleaning on each tooth. It took about five minutes. I watched and found myself actually losing interest as I daydreamed about Diego.

It was over practically before it started, and Dr. Brown sat me up all the way.

"How was it?" she asked with a smile.

"It's already over?" I asked.

She smiled and nodded. "Just a mini cleaning, remember?"

"Thanks!" I said, and I couldn't help it. I threw my arms around her for a huge hug. I was so relieved that I had survived, I felt ecstatic!

"You're welcome, my dear," she said, laughing and hugging me back hard. "You did very well!"

I practically floated out to the waiting room, where my mom looked at me with a nervous, inquiring look. I gave her a thumbs-up, like Diego had given me, and she broke into a big grin. "Great!" she said. "Well done!"

She and Dr. Brown chatted for a minute, then it was time to go.

But I wasn't quite ready. "Do you do prizes?" I asked shyly. I had to know.

"Of course! Right at the receptionist's desk, before you walk out," said Dr. Brown. "Lots of fun goodies in there."

"Can I say bye to Diego?"

"Absolutely. Let me check first that he's decent," she joked.

Then she called me in, and Diego was sitting there, now getting his teeth polished.

"Thanks so much, Diego," I said. "And thanks, Nina."

"My pleasure," said Nina with a smile.

"'Ine, 'oo," said Diego through a mouth full of toothpaste.

I waved good-bye and then went to check out the prizes. I mean, come on! What's the point of a job well done if you don't get a prize at the end?!

I selected a cute tattoo that said "Champ" on it

and they let Jake get a prize too. It was a tiny teddy bear dressed up like a policeman; kind of a junky little carnival prize, but he was thrilled with it.

I grinned on the way home as I realized that there was a fifth *D* now: Diego! It wouldn't be easy to tote him around to my appointments (ha!), but I could at least picture him while I was at them!

CHAPTER 6

Nice Nurse Nancy

So, let's just say that I shouldn't have counted my chickens before they hatched.

The next day after school, my mom asked me to accompany her to the hospital for Jake's preoperative meeting. She'd need my help to distract Jake while she listened to the doctor and then filled out a bunch of paperwork. I was feeling pretty confident after my semitriumph at Dr. Brown's, so I agreed. I also figured it would be another advantage for my go-see the next day if I knew where I was headed. Looking back, maybe Matt or Sam should have gone with them instead of me.

In the car the whole way there, Jake explained how this was a waste of a trip, because there was NO WAY he was getting his tonsils out, so why were we bothering to do this? My mother kept sighing heavily, having given up on trying to fight his every protest. I tried a few times to clarify things for him, but he was having none of it, and I could see why my mom was so defeated. I clammed up too and looked out the window while I pretended not to notice Jake putting his thumb in his mouth.

We got to the check-in desk, and Jake was busy *not* looking around. It was like he'd decided to pretend he wasn't there. (Despite my new training from Dr. Brown, I could relate.) We checked in at the front desk, and a nice nurse named Nancy came out to meet us and show us around.

"So, Jake, when you come in on Friday morning, it will be bright and early. You won't have time for any breakfast in the morning, but that's okay, because you'll want to save room for all the ice cream you'll be having later," Nancy explained.

But Jake wouldn't meet Nancy's eye. He pulled his policeman bear—his new sidekick—out of his pocket and began walking the bear along some paneling on the wall. The nurse turned to my mom and said quietly, so Jake couldn't hear, "He's scared, right?"

My mom nodded, exhausted, and the nurse patted her arm sympathetically. She continued on. "So, you'll come in here, where we'll get your pajamas on. . . ."

"Do we bring our own, or . . . ?" asked my mom.

"No, we'll give him a gown, actually. Then we put him on a gurney and—Hey, Jake! Listen, this is the fun part! You get a free ride on a bed with wheels!" Nancy said cheerily.

Jake looked up, momentarily tricked. A ride on a bed sounded great! But then he remembered where we were and why, and he frowned and looked away again. The nurse and my mom exchanged glances.

"Then we'll go to the lab and get a quick little prick for a blood test," said Nancy.

My ears pricked at the sound of the word "blood," but there was no time to adjust my thinking, because right then we turned a corner and into the lab, and the room was actually full. There were two adults with bags of blood either dripping into or being sucked out of their veins, and a kid having blood taken. He had a rubber band around his arm, and the nurse was capping vials to the needle thingy and filling them with black-red blood.

Uh-oh!

I tried to think fast: Diego! Deep breaths! Mona! Divine! But it was all too much and too fast for my system. Definitely *not* divine.

I fainted.

When I came to, I was lying on a gurney, and my mom and Jake were peering anxiously at me. Nancy came bustling up with a glass of orange juice and a cool cloth for my forehead.

"I'm *so* sorry!" she apologized. "I wish I'd known! I never would have taken you there!"

I sighed heavily. "It's my fault. Mind over matter," I muttered.

"I am *not* having my tonsils out!" declared Jake.

"Oh boy," said my mom, putting her head in her hands. The nurse rubbed her back kindly. I closed my eyes.

It took a while for me to get my feet back under me. Usually, if I catch myself before I actually faint, I recover pretty quickly. But if I go all the way down, like I did this time, I'm kind of exhausted afterward. While I recovered, Jake sat on the end of my gurney and played with his officer bear. Meanwhile, Nancy outlined all the procedures for my mom and had her sign waivers and permissions for tests and medication and aftercare and all kinds of things. When we finally left, I think we all felt like we'd been there for a week. Nancy insisted on riding me out in a wheelchair, saying it was hospital policy. I felt ridiculous and hoped I wouldn't see anyone I knew.

But wouldn't you know it, as we reached the exit, the doors slid open, and there was Olivia Allen with her mother.

She looked at me, and her eyes widened.

"I'm fine!" I said by way of greeting, then added, "Hospital policy."

Olivia looked at me searchingly. "Wait, are you already done with the go-see?" she asked with such confusion that I had to laugh. I'd forgotten all about the go-see for the time being.

"No, I'm . . . I was just here with Jake, he's having his tonsils out, so we were here for a tour. . . ."

"Emmy fainted," Jake announced cheerfully.

"What?" said Olivia, aghast. "Are you okay?"

I tried to smile brightly. "Don't exaggerate, Jake. I think the go-see's tomorrow, though, right?" I asked Olivia, changing the subject.

She nodded, all business now. "We're just here for a dry run, to get the lay of the land," she reported. "We thought we'd walk around a little, get used to the sights and sounds. . . ."

She looked at her mother, who had pressed her lips together into a thin line. Her mom is so competitive and critical of Olivia, she was probably trying to send Olivia a sign to be quiet, lest she give the competition (me) an advantage or leg up of some sort. Ha! She needn't have worried. I had all the info I needed, believe me. In fact, if you'd asked me right then and there, I would have told Olivia the job was hers and good riddance to that hospital. I'd never be back.

"I'm sorry, girls, but we need to move along now," said my mom. "This nice lady needs to get back to work." She glanced at Nancy.

Nancy had been following the conversation. "Are you girls coming here tomorrow for something?" she asked.

Olivia nodded. "It's a go-see for the hospital's publicity office," she said, drawing herself up straight. "We're models."

"Oh, what fun!" said Nancy. "I can see that, now that you mention it." She smiled at me. Olivia kind of coughed, but Nancy didn't say anything to her. "Well, I sure hope it doesn't have anything to do with blood!" We sailed out the door, leaving Olivia and her mom with confused looks on their faces.

My mom and I couldn't help it. We got into the car and started laughing, and we could not stop. It was nerves and we knew it, but Jake didn't understand, and he was getting frustrated. "What's so *funny*?" he kept demanding, and of course that only made us laugh harder.

"Oh boy!" said my mom finally, wiping tears of laughter from her eyes. "And we're coming back here tomorrow? *And* again on Friday?" We started laughing all over again.

That night, as I lay in my bed, waiting in the dark for my parents to come say good night, I thought hard about the modeling job. First of all, I really needed the money. I was broke, and I was tired of having to pass on all the things I wanted, like the shirt at Icon and the yummy breakfast cereal. Just a little spending money would be nice. Also, I needed to pay back the Cupcake Club for losing that money from The Special Day bridal salon. Second of all, I had committed to showing up for the job, and I really couldn't back out at the last minute. It would be unprofessional, and I wouldn't want to earn a bad reputation after I'd worked so hard for a good one. And third of all, I couldn't stand to have Olivia Allen beat me out of a modeling job. I'd never hear the end of it. I knew number three was a lame reason, but I couldn't help it!

When my mom came in to kiss me, she said,

"So we're off for tomorrow, right? No need to put ourselves through that again."

"I don't know . . . ," I said. I hesitated and thought hard. I didn't want to go, but I felt like I should.

My mom reached up to turn my bedside reading light on. I squinted at her in the sudden brightness as she looked hard at me. "Emma, I know that modeling is wonderful work for you, and the income is lovely. I have really come around to it, despite my initial misgivings, mostly because of how well you handle it. I don't want to be your agent or be a stage mother in any way. But I have to ask: Do you really think this is a good idea?"

"Well, I don't want to let anyone down, like . . . professionally. I want to be known as reliable. And also I really need some money."

"What for? How much?" asked my mom.

"Um . . . I absolutely have to have forty dollars to pay back the Cupcake Club for that money I lost. And then, well, I just have no cash. No pocket money right now."

My mom looked up at the ceiling. "How about if Dad and I front you the money for the club payback. I will have you pay us back for that when you make some money, since it was careless that you lost it, and I won't cover carelessness. Also, I can't

66

imagine there's any product you can't live without for a while, like clothes or apps or whatever, until you earn a little more cash to buy it yourself. But if there are any outings you need money for, like pizza and the movies, Dad and I will cover you until you get some more work, okay?"

That all sounded fair. Now I just felt guilty and nervous about my reputation. "Won't it look bad if I cancel the day of the go-see?"

My mom puffed out her lips and thought. "Look, if you were terrified of sharks, would you go down and do a shoot in a shark cage?" she asked.

"No way!"

"Okay, well, for now, blood is your shark. And you've certainly been trying hard to get yourself over it. It's just not going to happen that fast. I'll just call Alana and explain it. Maybe she has someone else they could use. Okay?"

I felt a huge weight lifted off my shoulders. I snuggled deep into my covers and started to fall asleep immediately, I was so relieved. "Okay, Mama," I said, calling her by my private baby name for her.

"Good night, my little worker bee," she said, kissing the top of my head. I was so sleepy, I didn't even remember her closing the door.

CHAPTER 7

Vampire Cupcakes

At lunch the next day, I slid into my seat and handed Alexis a white business envelope with forty dollars in it.

"Thanks," she said. "But, wait. Did you get an advance on the modeling job?"

I had to laugh. "Alexis! You're so sharp, you even keep track of *my* finances?"

She rolled her eyes at me. "It's just the way my brain works. I can't help it!"

"My mom lent me the money. I'm not going," I said. I busied myself with putting a straw into my milk. I could feel Alexis staring at me.

"Wait, you bagged the job?" she asked.

Alexis and I both have very strong work ethics. The idea of not delivering on a job is inconceivable to both of us. Our professionalism is certainly a strong part of our friendship, and it's the backbone of the Cupcake Club. If we promise, we deliver.

I looked away as I sucked from the mini milk container, stalling for time. Finally, I said, "I couldn't get over the blood thing fast enough. I fainted at the hospital yesterday on Jake's preop tour."

Alexis's jaw dropped in shock, right as Mia and Katie slid into places across the table.

"What?" asked Mia.

"What did we miss?" insisted Katie, her eyes dancing merrily.

"I fainted at the sight of blood yesterday, so I can't go to the modeling job today."

"Whaaaat? After all your hard work?" said Katie.

"All your *mom's* hard work, for nothing!" I said grimly. "I feel bad."

"Well, you got to watch Diego Diaz get his teeth cleaned." Katie giggled. "So it wasn't all for nothing!"

We all started to laugh. "He *is* a cutie!" I said.

"So, now what?" asked Mia, eating her chili.

"Well, I'll try to get some more go-sees, pay my parents back. Probably write a note of apology to the publicity person at the hospital . . ."

"No, silly, not your career! Now what with

Diego!" Mia laughed, and we all started laughing again. I didn't have an answer for her, so the topic quickly turned to Jake's send-off the next afternoon. Now that my go-see was canceled, I could come help bake today.

"Are you sure you want to be a part of the vampire cupcakes?" asked Katie in concern.

I nodded through my spaghetti. "Mmm-hmm," I said. Then I swallowed. "Fake blood doesn't bother me *that* much. Baking for a brat does, though."

"Ooh, poor Jake!" said Mia.

"No, poor *me*!" I corrected her.

That afternoon we baked at Alexis's house, which is close enough to my house to walk. We agreed that I would bring Jake's party cupcakes home tonight, since the other girls were on bikes, and we'd be all ready for Jake's little party tomorrow. Katie and Mia were whispering about a little present they'd gotten him, but they knew I was annoyed with all things Jake lately, so they didn't really discuss it in front of me. They knew I'd probably just roll my eyes or something.

It was fun just chilling with the girls in an all-girl house for the afternoon for a change. We wound up playing some of our silly cupcake games while we waited for the treats to cool, like Name That Cupcake.

"Okay, okay, how about pineapple upside-down cake . . . with hibiscus frosting . . . and flowered cupcake papers?" said Mia, her eyes twinkling.

"Oh! I know! Hula-Hoppers!" said Katie.

"Hula-*Hoppers*?" we cried, incredulous.

"That's awful, Katie!" said Alexis.

"Hula . . . Poppers?" she amended, and that made us laugh even harder.

"More like Hula-Floppers," said Alexis wryly.

"Wait, now I've got one," I said. "Golden yellow butter cake, with . . . butter crunch bits . . . dipped in buttercream frosting . . . and some fresh blueberries on top."

"Ooh, you had me until the blueberries," said Alexis. "How about Blueberry Fool?"

I smiled.

"Blueberry Crumble?" asked Katie.

"Blueberry Mumble?" joked Alexis, now that we were on the rhyming track.

"Wait! I have a great idea!" said Mia. "Let's play Name That Guy! We describe a guy, then see if people can guess his name!"

"Okay, I'll go first: short, bratty, obsessed with policemen . . . ," I said.

71

"No, just do guys our age!" said Mia, laughing.

"Athletic; curly hair; very, very blue eyes; great graphic designer . . .," said Alexis dreamily. We all knew she was describing my brother Matt.

"Alexis!" teased Katie. "That's too easy!"

So I said, "I have one: brave, cute, very white teeth . . ."

"Diego Diaz!" they all yelled in unison.

"Okay, maybe this game is too easy." Mia laughed.

While Katie mixed up the fake blood—raspberry sauce, I busied myself elsewhere, making the frosting and prepping the carrying container. I didn't have to see the "blood" at all, which was a relief. Despite what I'd said earlier, even listening to them talk about it made me feel queasy.

"Oh, it's so realistic," said Alexis. Katie had mixed in a little cornstarch to thicken the sauce. I peeked, and she was dipping a spoon into the mixture to taste it. "Yum!" I quickly looked away.

"Katie, wow! That looks really good. Maybe you should go into special effects!" said Mia approvingly.

Even without looking, I couldn't take much more. So while Katie filled the cooled cupcakes ("You wield a mean syringe, Dr. Brown!" teased Mia), I called my mom at work to see how her call with Alana went. The go-see would have been well under way by now.

"Hi, honey," she said. "It's all taken care of."

"How did it go?" I asked, squeezing my eyes shut in dread.

"Actually, they were very nice about it. It turned out there was some sort of glitch with the other model too, so they just decided to scrap it for today after all. They said to call back if you change your mind, since they're not sure when they'll end up shooting it."

"I don't think I will change my mind, though," I said. "Is that okay?"

"Of course! Please, sweetheart! I just thought it was nice they offered to keep the door open."

"Yeah," I said. "I wonder if the other model was Olivia Allen? And if so, I wonder what happened with her schedule? She certainly seemed excited for the job."

"I don't know. Maybe she wasn't comfortable with it either. She probably canceled. Who knows?" said my mom.

I had a hard time picturing Olivia not following through on a job. She wanted to be a model so badly, she would have walked over hot coals for the work.

"So, you'll be home in time for dinner?" she asked.

"Yup. Almost done. When will you be home?"

"A little late since we have our staff meeting tonight. Maybe you could start the rice for me at six?" she asked.

"Oh, right! I forgot about your meeting. Sure, I can do that."

"Okay, sweet pea. Thanks. And thanks for checking in. Love you!"

"Love you, too. Bye!"

I hung up the phone and then stared at the receiver. I wondered for a second if I should call Olivia, to see if everything was okay. I mean, there is no way that girl would back out of a job. Not with her ego. But I decided against it. I really wasn't friends with her, and I didn't want to be nosy. I'd ask her at school tomorrow if I ran into her.

We finished up Jake's cupcakes and packed them into the carrier, and I headed home shortly after. I put the cupcakes on the top shelf of the pantry, where Jake wouldn't find them, and I headed upstairs to take a shower and then start my homework. I was sitting at my desk in my pj's, with a towel-turban wrapped around my head, when I remembered about the rice. I hopped up and then skipped downstairs toward the kitchen. But as I got near the kitchen, something caught my eye. There were little puddles on the floor; wet splotches of . . . blood?

No one was home but me, Matt, and Jake. Matt had been in his room the whole time, and Jake had been watching TV and hadn't made a peep. I could hear the TV playing from the TV room behind me, but I didn't want to scare Jake, so I let him be.

"Matt?" I said quietly. I was now scared for real as my brain replayed every late-night true-crime show I'd ever seen about intruders. "Jake?" But he didn't reply either. I *really* didn't want to go into the TV room and alarm him, so I kept going.

I reached the kitchen door and nervously peered around the corner. It was dark, and there was no one there. I grabbed a pair of sharp kitchen scissors from the butcher block and followed the blood stains as they continued past the kitchen and toward the front of the house.

"Matt? Jake?" I called again softly, but I heard nothing. The stains led to the front hall and then stopped, right outside the front hall closet. It was dark there too, and I couldn't decide whether to flick on the light or confront the intruder in the dark. My heart was pounding so fast, I almost felt like I could see it. I decided I needed the element of surprise on my side, so I put one hand on the closet's doorknob and one on the light switch. I held the scissors in the light-switch hand, so I'd be ready to thrust them into the intruder if he or she came at me.

Okay, deep breaths, I told myself. In through my nose, out through my mouth. Think of Mona. Think of Diego.

"Hi-*yahh*!" I yelled, flinging open the closet door and flicking on the light. I jumped into ready position, my scissors held aloft like a samurai sword. My adrenaline was coursing through my veins, my heart pumping: I was ready to take on anyone! Anyone except . . .

"Jake?"

"Emmy," he said. His face was covered in blood, and he was crunched up in a ball, lying on the floor of the closet under all the long coats, his police officer bear clutched tightly in his hand.

My knees gave out at the sight of all the blood, and I dropped to the floor. "Jake! Are you okay?" I cried.

He sat up woozily and looked at me in confusion. "Am I in trouble?" he asked.

Despite *my* wooziness, I was so scared, I kept

functioning. "No! Why would you be in trouble? What *happened* to you? Is it your tonsils? Did you try to take them out yourself? OMG! Come out here, so I can see you! Can you walk?"

Jake crawled out of the closet and sat back on his haunches. "Emmy, you're not mad?"

"Mad! Why would I be *mad*? You're lucky to be alive!" I cried. Jake's whole shirtfront was soaked with blood. I tried to stay calm, like Mom and Dad taught me to do if there was an emergency. "Come, quick, to the kitchen. I'll call Mom. Wow, actually, we might have to call an ambulance. That's a lot of blood. Quick! *Matt!*" I hollered. "Get down here quick!"

"I feel sick," said Jake. "I can't walk."

"MATT!" I screeched. "Help us! Jake's been attacked or something!"

Matt came bounding down the stairs two at a time. "What is it?" he yelled. Then he saw Jake. "What the—? Jake! What did you do?" He ran to Jake's side, crouching down next to him on the rug.

"I . . . I . . ." Jake started to cry.

Matt and I looked at each other in fear.

"I ate all the cupcakes!" Jake wailed.

"What?" Now Matt looked at me in confusion. "What does that mean?"

Suddenly, it all came together. "Jake, you ... Oh! The vampire cupcakes. Jake! You ate the cupcakes in the carrier I hid in the pantry?"

Jake nodded and wailed even louder.

I sat back against the wall, relief flooding me. And then I started to laugh. I reached out and wiped a streak of blood off Jake's cheek and I put it to my tongue. Yup. Red raspberry sauce. I started to laugh hysterically. What a fool I was!

"You people are freaks," said Matt in disgust. "You're telling me this kid ate a bunch of those creepy, vampire cupcakes and you thought he was hacked up by a mad man? You both need help. Major help." He shook his head and stood up. "Mom's going to kill you, Jake, for what you did to the rug."

"I'm going to throw up," Jake said. He began to cry.

"Run!" I yelled, and Jake jumped to his feet and, luckily, made it to the bathroom in time.

"I might puke too," I said to Matt.

"I might puke from the two of you," he said. "Couple of weirdos." He climbed the stairs to his room.

"Oh boy," I said out loud. "Time for a new recipe."

Gingerly, I lifted the police officer bear from the closet floor with two fingers and took him to the kitchen to wipe away the raspberry blood from his uniform. He looked like he'd been injured in the line of duty, which I suppose, for a toy bear, he had been.

CHAPTER 8

Jake in the Doghouse

𝒟inner was late that night, and Jake's cupcake party for the next day was canceled. My mom had had it with him and said it was time to stop playing Mrs. Nice Mom and start playing Mrs. Tough Mom. She had Jake help her clean the rug (not a huge success), then she ran him a bath and sent him to bed without dessert or a bedtime story.

My dad was happy that my mom had finally seen the light and stopped babying Jake, so he was in a jolly mood at dinner. I was somewhat traumatized by the whole experience: the sight of the blood, the idea of an intruder, and my shock at seeing Jake covered in blood.

Matt was a little traumatized too, even though he wouldn't admit it. I know it freaked him out to see Jake like that, especially since Jake's been driving him so crazy lately. And you'll never believe this, but when I went upstairs after dinner, I saw Matt sitting on the side of Jake's bed, chatting quietly with him. I couldn't stop to eavesdrop—they would have seen me, and Matt would have left—so I just kept walking down the hall to my room. But I would have killed to know what Matt was saying. Whatever it was, I knew for sure that Jake was eating it up.

At school the next day, I told the Cupcakers what had happened last night, and I broke the bad news about Jake's party. Mia and Katie were really disappointed, but Alexis laughed.

"That kid really has some nerve, doesn't he?" she asked admiringly.

I laughed too. "You've got to hand it to him. He gets what he wants."

"It's not easy being the youngest of four," Mia protested protectively.

"It's pretty cushy. Trust me," I said.

"Can we stop by to wish him good luck and bring him his present, anyway?" asked Katie.

I shrugged. "I guess so. That's really nice of you."

"The poor little guy," cooed Mia.

"Wait. Stop," I said, holding my palm out in

front of me. "Don't do the poor-little-guy thing when you see him, because he's been hamming it up, and my mom said we're not helping him by babying him. We're just making him suspicious, like it's a bigger deal than we're telling him. The tonsils thing is just something that needs to be done, and the more businesslike we are about it, the better, which is what my dad has been saying all along."

"Okaayyy . . . ," said Mia.

I spied Olivia from across the cafeteria. The suspense was killing me. "Hang on a sec, you guys," I said, and I rose and crossed the room to meet her.

"Hey!" I said, tapping her on the shoulder, friendly.

"Hey," she said, glancing up, not as friendly. She turned back to her lunch.

I stood there for a second. I could tell she was hoping I'd walk away, but I wasn't going to. Not without the information I needed. "So what happened yesterday?" I asked.

Olivia shrugged and took a bite of her sloppy joe. "Nothing," she said, her mouth full.

"I mean, why didn't they end up doing the go-see?" I asked.

Olivia looked at me, as if sizing me up, then she said breezily, "It was canceled."

I was confused. "But why?"

She looked at me again, like, *Are you joking that you don't know?* But then she said dismissively, "I don't know," like, *That's all, now you can run along.*

I looked at her for an extra second. "Okay," I said. "Weird. Well, are they rescheduling it?"

Now Olivia was annoyed. "Honestly, I don't know. They were a little unprofessional. It was definitely an amateur go-see, so when they call back, I will be turning them down." She took another bite of her sandwich and then struck up a conversation with Bella, who was sitting next to her.

Huh.

I walked slowly back to my table, no more enlightened than I'd been on the phone with my mom yesterday. I guess it all worked out for the best, anyway, whatever had happened.

That afternoon, Mia, Katie, and Alexis came over. Jake was at the kitchen table doing his homework, his little police officer bear sitting on the table next to his workbook. He was banned from TV until after the operation, and my mom said she'd rethink his viewing privileges once he had recovered. She admitted we'd all been relying on the television as a babysitter (her fault, she said), and Jake needed more supervision, more human interaction, and less *SpongeBob*. She felt TV was making him bratty. I had to agree.

Anyway, the girls came in and shyly presented Jake with a wrapped gift box.

"I'm sorry I ate all the cupcakes for the party," he said, hanging his head.

"Oh, Jake!" said Mia, rushing to his side and giving him a big hug. "I heard all about it! You poor—" She looked up, and I was glaring at her, so she quickly changed course. "Well, that was a bad idea," she said, "but we forgive you." She hugged him again and tousled his hair.

"Sounds like you really scared Emma," said Alexis.

Jake nodded sadly. "I was a bad boy."

I rolled my eyes. Katie and Mia were ready to sweep him up and take him home, but I knew he was just hamming it up for them. He didn't really feel bad. Alexis caught my eye and winked. "You owe us $12.49 for the ingredients," said Alexis.

Jake's head snapped up, and he looked at her. "Really?"

"No!" She laughed. "Just kidding!"

Jake grinned. "Because I do have seven dollars. . . ."

"Keep your money, kiddo. What kind of an account do you have it in?" asked Alexis.

"Alexis!" we all cried in unison.

She put up her palms and laughed. "Whoa! Sorry! I was just going to give the kid a little business advice."

My mom came in from the den where she'd been working and said, "I heard all the laughing, so I had to come see what was going on!"

Despite the fact that we weren't allowed to have a party for Jake, the gathering had a festive air, and when Mom said he could open his present, he was excited. We watched as he slit open the gift wrap (much more controlled than his usual present-tearing frenzy) and graciously read the card before whipping open the box. He was still trying to be on his good behavior around me and my mom, I could see.

"'Dear Jake, good luck! We love you! Love, the Cupcake Club XOXO.'"

"But the hugs and kisses aren't from me," I joked.

"Emma!" whispered Mia, hiding a smile.

Jake lifted the lid, and inside was a navy blue T-shirt designed to look like a police officer's uniform. He held it up and yelled, "Look! It's a real police shirt!"

"Look at the back," instructed Katie, who was excited.

He spun it around and read," 'Officer Jake Taylor'! It's awesome! Thank you!"

Jake stood and put the shirt on over what he was wearing. It was a little bit big, but not too bad, and the smile on his face was truly gratifying. "I love it! Thank you!" He went around and hugged my three friends, who ate it up.

"Wow, Jake, that's a really nice present," said my mom.

"We thought it would be comfy to lounge around in during your recovery," said Alexis.

"My recovery from what?" asked Jake.

Alexis's face reddened. "Oh, um, your tonsils?" She looked at me, as if to say, *What? Did I say something wrong?*

I rolled my eyes and shook my head.

"Oh, I'm not doing that anymore," Jake said calmly.

Mia and Katie exchanged looks of confusion, while my mother gathered up the box and said briskly, "Jake, please thank the girls again, and then it's time to finish your homework."

Mia and Katie stood, both of them saying "Well . . ." at the same time and then laughing.

"Thanks, Emma! Bye, Jake," said Alexis.

"I'll walk you out," I said.

"Bye, girls! Thanks!" said my mom.

Outside, my friends were confused. "Wait, so he is or he isn't having the operation?" asked Mia.

"Oh, he's having it," I said.

"So what was that all about?" asked Alexis.

I exhaled heavily. "I don't know. I think he's just toying with my mom or something. Or maybe he really thinks he can back out. All I can say is, I'll be glad once I'm at school tomorrow morning and this is all behind me."

But little did I know how the next twenty-four hours would unfold.

Only hours later, Matt, Sam, and I were hunkered down in the TV room with the door closed and the baseball game blaring on the TV, but it still didn't drown out the wails coming from upstairs.

"If that kid's tonsils weren't shot before tonight, they're definitely gone after all that screaming," said Sam, shaking his head.

I looked over at Matt and realized he was wearing what we call "homework headphones"— the kind you use for noise reduction at car races and stuff. "Nice touch," I said.

"What?" he said, looking at me blankly.

I jabbed my thumb in Matt's direction and grinned at Sam.

Sam shook his head and laughed. "Yeah, he looks like a total geek, but don't you wish you had some?"

"What?" Matt repeated.

Sam lifted one of the earphones off the side of Matt's head and yelled into Matt's ear. "You can't have it both ways, dude!" Matt pulled away and swatted Sam.

"Either be part of the conversation or don't!" yelled Sam.

I laughed as Matt punched him in the arm.

Suddenly, Jake came racing into the room, wild eyed and crying hysterically. "Hide me, Emmy!" he shrieked. "I'm not going tomorrow!"

Even though we were all sick of the show he'd been putting on and the way my parents had let him get away with so much bad behavior, Matt and Sam and I exchanged uneasy glances. We *did* feel bad for the kid.

I scooped him onto my lap, and he burrowed against my neck, his little police officer bear clutched tightly in his hand. He wrapped his arms around me and held tight. It reminded me of when he was a little baby and my mom would sometimes let me give him his bottle. He'd snuggle in and fall asleep in my arms. It was pretty cute.

But then my parents were at the door, and it wasn't cute.

"Jake, it's time for bed," said my mother in her most no-nonsense voice.

"No!" he yelled.

Sam and I rolled our eyes at each other. Matt just kept watching the TV.

"Jacob William Taylor, it is time for bed and I do not want one peep out of you!" yelled my father in the scary voice he only uses about three times a year. "Now, march!"

We all know what that voice means, so Jake did as he was told, but reluctantly and very slowly.

"Let's go, pick up the pace," ordered my father. Jake hurried up so slowly, it was hardly noticeable. My mom stood and watched, her arms folded tightly across her chest. My father hustled him along, out the door and up the stairs. My mom, meanwhile, collapsed onto the sofa next to me.

"I cannot wait for this to be over." She sighed.

I patted her arm. "Poor Mama," I said.

"Listen, guys—Hey, Sammy, mute the TV for a second, okay? Matt? Matt?" She reached out and tapped his leg, and he jumped. "Earphones off, honey, just for a minute."

Matt lifted the headphones off his head and put them in his lap.

"Okay, here's the plan for tomorrow. Dad and Jake and I are leaving very early for the hospital in the morning. You'll have to fend for yourselves, so please make sure your alarms are set, and first one up, wake up the others, just in case. There's cereal for breakfast or whatever you want to make; just please don't leave the kitchen a mess. Jake heads in at nine for the surgery. It should take about an hour. We'll text you when it's all over and let you know how it goes. There's a very slight possibility they'll keep him overnight, in which case Dad or I will come home, grab a bag, and go back to stay with him. I'm bringing a bag for him, anyway, just in case."

"Oh, I have something for him. Can I put it in the bag?" asked Sam.

"Sure. That's nice of you, honey," she said.

Sam hopped up and went to get it.

"I have something for him too," said Matt, and he left the room.

I looked at my mom. "I don't have anything!" I admitted guiltily.

"Oh, honey, you do so much for him. Don't worry. Anyway, now he has that little bear that he loves from Dr. Brown's office. He wouldn't have had that if it wasn't for you. Same with the cute T-shirt from the girls."

"And don't forget the vampire cupcakes!" I chimed in.

My mom put her head in her hands. "How could I forget the vampire cupcakes! My rug will never forget the vampire cupcakes either!"

Sam reappeared with a card that said "JAKE" on the front of the envelope.

"That's so thoughtful, Sammy," said my mom.

"They're passes for the movie theater. I said I'll take him next week when he feels up to it."

"What a great idea!" said my mom.

Then Matt came back. He had done a clumsy wrapping job on some sort of spherical object. "Here. It's a baseball. I also stuck in a coupon good for one hour of playing catch with me."

My mom reached out and grabbed Matt for a kiss on the cheek. "Wonderful. You boys are so thoughtful. I'm proud of you," she said, smiling.

"What did you get him, Em?" asked Sam with a proud smirk.

"Nothing," I said, my shoulders sagging.

"It's not too late!" said Sam. "Want me to run you down to the drugstore?" Sam's got a new used car that he bought from a friend, so he's always offering to drive people places.

"That's so lame! What would I get him? Something to gargle with afterward?"

Matt smiled.

"Emma, don't be ridiculous. You're not running out at nine o'clock at night to get Jake a present. You've done more than enough for him. If you really feel like you want to give him something, I have a new pack of markers and a fresh pad of drawing paper I was saving to give him at the hospital tomorrow. Why don't I say it's from you?"

"Fine. Thanks," I said. "I still feel lame."

"Oh boy. I'm going to bed!" said my mom, standing up. "I'll be upstairs, and I want you guys in bed at the regular time. I know tomorrow's a Friday, but you've got to get some rest too, okay?"

"Night, Mama," I said, reaching up for a hug. She kissed my head and then the boys', and she left.

"Slacker," Matt said to me as soon as she was gone.

"Shush!" I said, and I unmuted the game.

CHAPTER 9

The Big Day

I was sound asleep and dreaming that little frogs were hopping up my arms. Only it wasn't a dream. I opened my eyes, and the frogs weren't frogs but Jake's fingertips, patting up and down my arm to wake me up. And Jake's face was about three inches from mine, his sleepy little boy breath right in my nose.

"Jake! What time is it?" I bolted upright, avoiding Jake's head by a millimeter, and looked at the clock. Three in the morning! "What's the matter?" I asked urgently.

"Emmy, I'm scared," said Jake. "Can I come in bed with you?"

"Did you wet the bed?" I asked. Sometimes that happens, and I didn't want a wet kid in my bed. Gross.

"No. I'm dry. I'm just really, really scared," he said. And, in fact, he sounded it.

I didn't hesitate. "Sure," I said, holding up my duvet so he could scramble in.

"Mmm, it's so warm in here!" he said.

"That's because I was asleep!" I retorted, wanting to be asleep again.

Jake snuggled in next to me. "Thanks, Emmy," he said sleepily. "I don't want to go tomorrow."

"I know," I said.

"It's going to hurt," he said.

"I know," I replied. (What could I do? Lie?)

"I wish I didn't have to do it," he confessed.

"I know," I said, yawning.

"Would you do it if you were me?" he asked quietly.

"Mm-hmm," I said.

"Yes?" he asked in a tiny voice.

"Yes," I said, and although I wanted to drift back to sleep, suddenly my brain was wide awake, and I was starting to worry. It was like Jake passed his worry off to me, so he could go to sleep and I'd stay up and do the worrying!

Here's the thing: My mom said the surgery was routine and easy, but . . . My stomach clenched as I played out worst-case scenarios in my mind.

tests, nothing. And I haven't missed one day yet this year!"

"Oh, Emma . . . ," said my mom.

But Jake stopped crying, like someone had just turned off a faucet. "Yes. Emma's coming with me!" he yelled. He wasn't exactly cheery, but it was like he seized on the idea for some reason and now he started to beg. "Please, Mom, let Emmy come!"

"Fine, but let's go!" snapped my dad.

My mom and I looked at each other and shrugged. I hopped out of bed, grabbing Jake by the shoulders. "No more nonsense, okay? If you start this up again, I won't come, do you understand?"

He sniffled and nodded.

"Even at the hospital!" I said firmly.

He nodded again, and then he grabbed me into a hug. "Oh, Emma! I love you!"

"Love you too, buddy, now get out so I can change."

He left, and I whipped off my pj's and threw on some sweats and a soft T-shirt, plus a pair of cushy socks and my slides. I jammed a couple of books into my backpack and grabbed my phone from the charger.

In the hall I ran into Matt stumbling sleepily to the bathroom.

"Sorry, gotta go first!" I said, ducking in front of him.

"What?" said Matt crankily. "Why?"

"Going to the hospital with Jake," I said, closing the door on Matt's face.

"You're skipping school?" demanded Matt, pounding on the door.

"Sorry! Someone's in here!" I singsonged back.

He pounded the door once more, hard, and I jumped. Then I heard him trudging down the hall to my parents' bathroom, calling "Unfair!" over his shoulder. I smiled at myself in the mirror as I brushed my teeth, but my smile faded as I pictured being back at the hospital. Mind over matter. The five Ds. Mona. Diego. Divine. I took a deep breath to relax, but I was spitting out my toothpaste at the same time, causing me to nearly choke to death.

Okay, deep breathing when I get there, I told myself.

Down in the kitchen, Jake was on a new tirade because he couldn't find his officer bear to bring with him. My mom had run up to look through his room and mine, but no luck. My dad was ready to explode and had dragged Jake off to the minivan to wait for us while my mom shouted after him with promises of new toys from the gift shop.

My mom turned to me then and said, "Emma, we don't have time to eat. Dad will get you something at the hospital, but I don't think it's fair if we eat in front of Jake, since he can't. Why don't you grab something quick, like a yogurt, and you can eat it in the bathroom there or something, where Jake can't see you."

"Okay," I said, and instead of the fridge, I went to the drawer my mom stocks with cereal bars, so we can just grab them when we're heading out for sports or if we're late for school or something. I pulled it open, and there was the officer bear lying in the drawer.

"Mom," I called, and when she looked over at me, I wiggled the bear at her.

"Oh my goodness, Emma. What would we do with out you?" she asked, exhaling heavily. She put her hands palms down on the counter and bent her head for a moment. She was wiped out.

I grabbed a couple of cereal bars and tossed them into my backpack, then I went over and rubbed my mom's back.

"Thanks, honey. Let's go," she said, straightening up and grabbing her purse. "Oh, Emma?" She stopped in her tracks. "Are you sure this is a good idea? I don't want you to feel railroaded into something you're not comfortable with. I mean, it's generous of you and everything, but you're not going to . . . ?"

"I'm not going to faint, Mom. I promise," I said solemnly. Inside, though, I hoped I could keep that promise. Gulp.

"Good," said Mom. "Because I can only handle one kid losing it at a time."

Out in the car, Jake was buckled into his booster seat in the back. His eyes were red-rimmed and puffy, but at least he wasn't actively crying or shrieking for the moment. It seemed like he acted worse when he thought he had a chance to get out of something, but once he knew he was sunk for sure, he'd just kind of mellow out.

"Hey, buddy," I said, climbing in. I handed him the bear.

"Emmy! Where did you find him?" he asked, hugging the bear.

I shrugged. "In the cereal bar drawer."

"Bad bear, I told you not to eat anything before the hospital!" Jake scolded.

My mom and I smiled at each other in the rearview mirror as my dad backed down the driveway.

✿

Even though the streets were quiet, the hospital was very busy. It seemed more like noon than six thirty in the morning in there. I focused on my breathing and just kept reminding myself that this day wasn't about me. It was about Jake, so I owed it to him to remain calm and not steal the spotlight by fainting again. Nothing was going to happen to me as long as I didn't look in any doorways or too closely at any needles.

We checked in at the desk and were directed to the preop area. As we walked, Jake held my hand in one hand and clutched the officer bear in the other. His eyes were wide with fear, but he didn't cry, and my dad began to relax a little. The nurses were really nice, and they gave Jake a cute gown to wear with fire trucks all over it. (In a pinch, fire trucks are almost as good as police cars to Jake.) Then we had some downtime, and that was the hardest part.

My mom gave Jake the presents from Matt and Sam to kill some time, and then she gave him the one from "me." Naturally, Jake adored the boys' presents, and he wanted to play catch in the waiting area, but my parents wouldn't let him. So Jake and I drew and played hangman and tic-tac-toe until finally I was so hungry, I couldn't stand it, and I told

Jake I had to go to the bathroom, so I could hide down the hall and eat my cereal bar.

At this point, it was eight fifteen, and Jake would be called in at any minute. As I walked down the hall, a door to a doctor's office opened, and I heard a man's voice saying "See you in two weeks!" and out walked Diego Diaz and a man who must've been his dad!

"Diego!" I said, so surprised to see him that I blurted out his name before I even had a chance to feel shy.

"Hi, Emma," he said. He was not his usual happy self, though. "What are you doing here?"

"My little brother is getting his tonsils out, so I'm here for moral support," I said, shrugging. "Hi," I said to his dad. Diego introduced us.

"Oh! You're the model who's scared of the dentist!" said his dad, smiling genially.

"Dad!" said Diego, blushing. He rolled his eyes at me.

I felt bad for Diego, because obviously he'd told his parents about me, and now he was mortified. But I felt great for me, because Diego had found our dentist visit worth mentioning! Quickly, I said, "I know. It's crazy that I'm even here, because the last time I came as a visitor, I fainted! I can't believe

102

they even let me back in here!" I laughed.

Diego and his dad laughed too. "Well, I have to come back and get an operation on my ankle," said Diego, his smile fading as he thought of it. "I hurt it playing lacrosse, and it just keeps getting worse."

"That's a bummer," I said. "But maybe you'll be, like, bionic after!" I was trying to make him feel better.

He smiled. "I hadn't thought of it that way," he said. "Mostly I'm just dreading it."

"Well, you're much braver than I am. You were a rock star at the dentist's, anyway, where I would normally faint, so I think you'll handle this just fine."

"Thanks," said Diego.

We smiled awkwardly at each other for a minute, and then his dad cleared his throat and said, "I think we'd better head out, so you're not too late for school, son. It was nice to meet you, Emma. Good luck with your brother's tonsils!"

"Thanks!" I said, waving as they walked away.

"Bye," Diego called over his shoulder.

I couldn't believe Diego of all people was nervous about an operation. At Dr. Brown's, he was so cool. I guess everyone has something they're scared of (okay, maybe a few things). I was smiling happily to myself as I started walking again, lost in a daydream of Diego and me on a date at the movies. I wasn't paying much attention to my surroundings, and, suddenly, I turned a corner and found myself back at that dreaded lab room again, where I'd fainted the other day.

I gasped and ducked back around the corner I'd just turned, flattening myself against the wall. That room was like kryptonite for me! A passing nurse gave me a funny look and said, "Everything okay?"

I nodded and decided to eat my cereal bar right there. I was almost all the way through it when suddenly Jake and my parents appeared, with Jake riding in a wheelchair!

"Emmy! There you are!" he cried. "Look at me! I'm just like you were in the wheelchair! Woohoo!"

At least he was having fun for the moment.

"Is it time?" I asked my parents through my dry, sawdusty mouth.

"He's just going to the lab to get the port put in for the IV," explained my dad.

"You stay here," my mom said firmly to me.

"No! Emmy, come!" cried Jake in a baby voice.

"Oh, Jake, I can't go in there," I said sadly. "I'm not allowed."

But someone hadn't briefed the nurse. "Sure you are, honey. It's just fine. There's no one else in there yet, anyway," she said, peeking around the corner at the lab.

My mom and I groaned.

"See?" said Jake. "Come!"

"Oh, Jake . . ."

"Don't be scared, Emma. I'll be there to take care of you," he said. "You can hold my bear."

He was so cute, I almost cried. How could I put my own fears before his bravery and generosity? I took a deep breath, nodded at my mom, and said in a fake cheerful voice, "Okay! Let's go!"

In the lab, I tried to focus only on Jake's face. I didn't want to see any needles on the counter or vials of blood waiting for collection or anything. I didn't watch as the nurse snapped on her gloves and tied the rubber tube around Jake's arm. (Okay, I watched a little, but more like you'd watch a snake in the room with you: out of the corner of your eye, to make sure it doesn't attack.)

The nurse kept up her chatter the whole time, to distract Jake, but it kind of worked for me too. I kept trying to breathe in through my nose and out through my mouth like Dr. Brown taught me.

"So, how old are you, honey? What grade are

you in? What's your favorite TV show?"

Jake answered politely and stared at everything the nurse did, totally fascinated by all the equipment and not at all freaked out.

"What's your bear's name, honey?" asked the nurse.

"Well . . . ," said Jake. He didn't really call it anything except "the officer bear," which isn't really a name, I guess. He looked at the bear for a minute, and then he looked up at the nurse. "Emma," he said with a grin.

"No, the bear, honey, not your sister," said the nurse. She was doing something with a needle and Jake's hand, but I was studiously avoiding looking at either. My knees felt a little wobbly all of a sudden, but I pinched myself and tried some deep breaths. *I can do this, I can do this,* I chanted in my head. Deep breaths, desensitize, distract . . .

"No, the bear's name is Emma too!" said Jake. "Because I love her!"

Awwww! "Jake! That's so nice!" I said. Mia and Katie would have a field day with that one when I told them.

"Well, you obviously have a very nice sister. You're awfully lucky," said the nurse, focusing on Jake's hand.

"I have some brothers, too," said Jake. "But they're not as fun."

"Oh, Jake," I said. I wanted to reach over and hug him right then and there.

"Okay, Jake, it's going to be a little pinch, then that's it," the nurse promised. "You just look at your sister, who is going to make a funny face at you and make you giggle but not wiggle!"

Jake looked at me, and my stomach did a little flip-flop. This was it! I was terrified. I was standing there in the middle of the hospital, and it was . . . divine! *Yes,* I thought. *It is just divine.* And with that I took a big breath and made a crazy face at Jake, who started to giggle. I thought about what Alexis had told me: Putting a needle in, for a shot or a blood test or whatever, takes just a couple of seconds, and before it even starts to hurt, it's over. *I can do anything for three seconds,* I thought, *especially for Jake.* And sure enough, after about three seconds, it was all over. The needle was in his hand, ready for the IV hookup, and he hadn't even complained. I just didn't look at it.

"Well, sweetie, you're all done with the pinchy part. What a good boy you are! So brave!" praised the nurse, taping the port in place. "I bet you'll get lots of ice cream when you're done here today, won't you?" She beamed at him.

I had to admit I was pretty surprised with how well Jake was handling it all, now that we were here. I think my parents were too. We kept waiting for the other shoe to drop, as they say. For the real Jake to appear, but so far, since we'd gotten here, Jake had actually been perfect.

The nurse wheeled Jake out of the room, and I stood up to follow. For a second, I felt woozy, and I put my hand out to steady myself against the wall.

"Emma!" my mom said sharply.

"I'm fine," I said. "I am totally fine."

She continued to watch me as I struggled for a minute. The rushing sound came into my ears a tiny bit, but I took deep breaths and closed my eyes to make the stars at the edges disappear. I thought of Diego and Jake and how brave they both were, and I told myself, *Suck it up, Taylor!* After all, I wasn't even the one having something done to me! Getting mad at myself kind of got my adrenaline going, and I was able to straighten up. I shook my head and opened my eyes, and I was fine.

"I'm fine," I said again to my mom.

She looked at me skeptically. "Give me your hand," she ordered.

"I am fine!" I protested.

"I don't care. I can't deal with two kids in wheelchairs this morning, thank you very much," my mom said stubbornly.

"What*ever*," I said, matching her cranky tone, but I held her hand and walked out into the hall, where Jake, my dad, and the nurse were just turning the corner ahead of us.

I'd done it. I'd survived. Now it was Jake's turn.

CHAPTER 10

Phew!

Jake was not so happy when they told him he'd have to leave Emma the bear in the waiting area with us.

"No," he said, holding Emma tightly in his hands.

Uh-oh. Maybe this was the tantrum that had been on the horizon the whole time.

"I'm sorry, honey, but we don't want the bear to get lost. Sometimes they drop on the floor and we don't see them, and I know you won't want to leave her behind, right? Isn't she looking forward to some ice cream later, too?" the nurse said with a wink.

"I'll take care of her for you, Jake, okay?" I said.

We were all trying to avoid another tantrum.

And we were finally in the home stretch!

"Look, let me see her, just for a minute," I said.

Reluctantly, Jake handed me the bear, and I cradled her in my arm and snuggled her next to my neck. "Just like you and me last night, right? Just like when you were a baby and I used to give you your bottle, okay?"

Slowly, Jake nodded. "Okay," he said in a tiny voice.

"I'll take good care of her. I promise," I said.

Jake sighed. I could suddenly see that the kid was exhausted, and the operation hadn't even started. He'd probably been so nervous all along, he hadn't been sleeping well for days. No wonder he'd been so bratty. The poor guy.

"Are we ready?" asked a peppy, big nurse who appeared in the doorway, wearing a pink shower cap and a different kind of outfit.

"I think so!" said my mom, fake cheerful and obviously nervous as heck. My parents had agreed my mom would go with Jake, and my dad and I would go to the cafeteria to wait for her. Once they gave Jake the medicine that would make him fall asleep for the operation, she'd be kicked out of the operating room and come meet us.

"Good luck, Jake!" I said as they transferred

him onto a gurney in the hall. "Have fun on your flying bed ride!" I bent down and kissed him on the head.

He smiled weakly at me as the nurse put a shower cap over his head. I almost couldn't breathe, it made me so nervous, but not in a fainting way. Just terrified for Jake.

The nurse tucked him under the covers, and my dad gave him a tight hug and a kiss on the head. "Love ya, bud," he said, and I could see when he stood up that he was crying a little and that he didn't want Jake to see it.

My mom waved and took Jake's hand, heading off down the corridor with him.

My dad and I, without speaking, followed the signs to the cafeteria.

Once there, we went through the line with trays, and the only things that really appealed to me were a bowl of chicken noodle soup and some pudding. We paid and then took our trays to a corner where the TV was playing. Some kid was watching *SpongeBob,* and my dad and I were just happy for the distraction of it. But it also made me think of Jake. I propped Emma the Bear on the table to watch us, and then my dad and I ate in silence.

Suddenly, I realized something and laughed out loud.

"What?" asked my dad.

"I'm doing what Jake has been doing!"

"What's that?"

"I stayed home from school, I'm wearing my cozy clothes, eating soup and pudding, and watching *SpongeBob* with my stuffed animal."

"Huh," said my dad. "How do you like it?"

"I hate it."

"Well, the good news is, after this operation, he won't have to do that anymore," said my dad, eating his bacon, egg, and cheese sandwich.

We chewed in silence and watched the undersea creatures and their little dramas unfold. I could tell my dad was nervous, because he kept checking his watch and looking at the door. Also, his leg was tapping uncontrollably under the table. I guess we all have different ways of dealing with nervousness.

Finally, after what seemed like hours but was only twenty minutes, my mom walked in.

My dad hopped up and waved. "Over here!" he called, and she saw us and headed over, giving him a thumbs-up as she walked.

"They're in, the sedation went well, and they should be on their way. They said forty-five minutes to an hour," she said as she reached the table.

My dad exhaled. "Okay. What can I get for you to eat?"

"Just coffee, please. And something sweet. Maybe something with lots of chocolate in it. Surprise me." She smiled weakly.

"Mother! I'm shocked!" I joked.

"I need it," she said. "Comfort food. Ugh, I just want this all over with and for Jake to be fine and home, and then I will fall into my bed for fifteen hours. I cannot wait." She pulled back her hair from her face and tied it into a rubber band, and then she rested her chin on her hands. She looked young in a ponytail, but tired.

"I totally don't want to make this about me, but can you believe I didn't faint back there?" I grinned.

My mom shook her head slowly. "I couldn't believe it. You fought it off! I'm proud of you!"

"I'm actually really proud of Jake," I said. "Who would have thought after the show he's been putting on these past two weeks that he would rally."

My mom nodded. "You should have seen him with the surgeon, doing a thumbs-up and then counting backward as they put him under. . . ." A small sob caught in her throat. "Sorry. It's just scary," she apologized, blotting at her eyes with a paper napkin from the dispenser on the table.

"I know. And this is just tonsils. Thank goodness it isn't something more serious," I said.

"I know." My mom's shoulders sagged heavily.

My dad returned with three plates: a Danish, a fat swirly cinnamon bun, and a huge slab of chocolate cake, as well as my mom's coffee in a paper cup.

"Looks like they could use some cupcakes around here," I said. "I'll have to tell Alexis."

"As long as you're not the one making the deliveries," teased my mom.

"I think I'm on the way out of all that. Now when I have to think of someone I admire while they're taking my blood or whatever, I'll just think of Jake. He can be my little hero," I said.

"Oh, Em," said my mom, reaching out to pat my hand.

We sat quietly for a moment, staring at a new show that had come on TV. I spaced out as more people—hospital employees, mostly—filled the cafeteria around us, quickly grabbing breakfast and sitting at the tables to wolf it down.

Two pretty women about my mom's age sat next to us and smiled, and we smiled back. They obviously worked here, but weren't nurses, so just out of boredom, I started to eavesdrop on them to see if I could figure out what they did.

"Yes, so now we need a new agency, a whole new plan for the campaign," one was saying.

"It was a dumb idea to begin with," said the other lady. "I don't know why the board went for it. It's not fair to ask children to pose near hospital equipment and blood."

"Well, they wanted to play on the heart strings, you know. Remind people kids get sick too. Guilt them into donating blood . . ."

I looked at my mom and saw that she was listening too.

"Well, I think once they realized there weren't any kid models who'd sit for the shoot, they knew they had a problem. . . ."

I widened my eyes at my mom. They were talking about the blood drive poster! I was sure of it! My mom held her finger up at me, like, *Wait.*

"Well, there was the one girl . . ." They both started to laugh and shake their heads.

My mom chose that moment to turn to them.

"I am so sorry to be nosy, and I hope you don't mind me butting in, but something you said just caught my attention. Were you talking about the audition for the blood drive poster, where you were going to use child models?"

The women looked surprised but were friendly. "Why, yes!" said one. "Did you know about it?"

My mother gestured at me. "Well, my daughter, Emma, was called to come in for the shoot but ... she's a little squeamish...."

"I used to be squeamish!" I corrected her jokingly.

"Anyway, she just didn't think she could pull it off, so we canceled." The other ladies introduced themselves, and my mom turned her chair to chat with them better.

"Well, I'm certainly glad you knew your own limits," said one of the ladies. Her voice then dropped to a whisper. "We had one model come in and actually faint when they set up the shot and brought in the blood."

The other woman shook her head. "The whole idea of the shoot was terrible from the get-go," she said. "They fired the ad agency that cooked it up, you know."

"No!" said my mom, shocked.

The ladies nodded.

I couldn't resist. "What was the girl's name? Who fainted?"

The women looked at each other. "Isabella? Was it? Or ... No! Olivia! That's it!"

117

The other lady laughed. "Right, because her mother was so angry with her. *'Olivia! For goodness' sake, get up!'* she said, and the poor child was out cold on the floor."

The other woman covered her mouth with her hand. "Oh, we shouldn't laugh. It was terrible."

"You're not a friend of hers, are you?" asked the other woman, suddenly nervous at being rude.

"Oh, well. I just know her from . . . around," I said, and took a last sip of my soup. "She's okay," I added. I actually was feeling a little bad for Olivia.

"Well, maybe if they come up with another idea, Emma would be interested."

"Emma is your name?" one lady asked. "I'll have to remember that. You'd be perfect for any ad, dear."

"Thank you," I said.

"It was nice chatting with you. Good luck!" said my mom.

The ladies left to get back to work, and I laughed.

"So now you *are* my agent! Drumming up jobs for me!" I teased.

"Oh, stop! Wait, was that bad?" asked my mom, suddenly mortified.

"Oh, Mama. You are too cute," I said.

I thought about poor Olivia fainting on the floor. I was so glad that wasn't me. OMG. How mortifying! I guess that explained the dry run she and her mom were doing the day we ran into them at the hospital. Olivia was trying to desensitize too!

Just then, my mom's cell phone buzzed. "Oh! It's the doctor!" she said, jumping up. "That was fast! Hello?"

She listened and said a few words, mostly "Great" and "Thank you," while giving us a big thumbs-up and smiling. Then she said, "We're on our way," and she hung up.

"All done?" asked my dad, looking at his watch. It had only been half an hour.

"Yup! Apparently his tonsils were as big as golf balls. It only took a few minutes to get them out, and the doctor said Jake did great. They're about to bring him into recovery, and the sedation will wear off in a little while, so he thought we'd better get up there, in case Jake wakes up."

We all stood and smiled at one another.

"Phew!" I said.

"Phew!" echoed my dad, and he reached out to hug us both.

CHAPTER 11

Back to Normal

When Jake woke up, we were all gathered around his bed: me, my mom, my dad, and Emma the Bear. Jake was groggy, and he blinked his eyes and looked around.

"Hi, honey," said my mom, smoothing the hair back from his forehead.

"Where is Emma?" he whimpered in a small voice, crying a tiny bit.

"She's right here, all safe and sound!" I said cheerily, wagging the bear at him.

"Not . . . the bear. *You*, Emma!" He reached his arms out for me, and I leaned in for a big hug from him. Now I was the teary one.

"Thanks, little dude," I said.

"I missed you," he said, squeezing tightly.

I scrunched my eyes tight to remember this moment the next time I got impatient with Jake, and I hugged him back as hard as I thought was safe. When he let go, I stood up, and my parents were beaming at us.

"Oh! I'd better text the boys to let them know everything's okay," said my mom, and she began tapping away on her phone.

I checked my phone and saw I had about eight messages from the other Cupcakers, asking for status updates and reports, starting from six thirty this morning!

"Jake, you sure have a lot of people who care about you!" I laughed and then read him the messages. Then I too tapped out some updates and hit send.

"Ice . . . cream . . . ," croaked Jake.

My parents laughed. "That didn't take long!" said my dad.

"In a little bit they'll let us leave, and you can have all the ice cream you want at home!" said my mom brightly.

"Now!" rasped Jake.

Uh-oh.

A nurse came over with a dish and a spoon and said, "Here's a little ice cream, just for the moment.

It's just plain vanilla flavor, but I think you'll like the way it feels in your throat." Then she turned to us and whispered, "He'll be a little cranky this morning as the sedation wears off. Don't worry, though! He should be back to his usual adorable self by dinnertime!"

"Oh good," I said. I couldn't take any more cranky Jake!

It wasn't until lunchtime that they finally wheeled him out with us and a big packet of information and gargle packets and prescriptions for some medicine, trailing behind. I couldn't believe how much stuff was involved in one "routine" operation. Jake loved the wheelchair ride, but he was pretty tired. We were home by two o'clock, and my mom gave Jake some medicine and another small dish of vanilla ice cream and then put him down for a nap.

I texted the Cupcakers to see where the baking session was today. I'd be able to catch up with them now and help, so only an hour and a half later I was in Katie's kitchen, working on Mona's weekly order and the bachelorette party's vampire cupcakes.

"So tell the part again about when he woke up," said Katie, whipping the marshmallow cream.

I sighed. "Come on!"

"It's just so cute!" said Mia. "You're so lucky to have someone who worships you like he does!"

"Well, he doesn't worship me all the time," I pointed out.

"Enough of the time," said Mia.

"Yeah, but you don't want to see him when he's *not* worshiping her!" Alexis laughed.

"Ugh, Katie, I can't even look at that raspberry stuff," I said, wincing. "I think we need to retire the vampire cupcakes after today."

"The poor girl is traumatized," said Alexis.

"Remember how I said my mom's book club wanted to place an order?" said Mia. "Well, they're reading a vampire book now!"

Everyone laughed but Alexis, who was thinking hard. "Hey, we should have a 'Book Club Specialties' section on our website, where we suggest pairings of popular book club books with certain cupcakes!"

"Wow, that would be really cool!" said Katie.

"We should really brainstorm on this and come up with a few," said Alexis. "I seriously think it would be a great category for us. We do so many book clubs, anyway."

"Oh, Alexis, by the way. I think you should try to sell cupcakes to the hospital's cafeteria! Their baked goods are so pathetic looking," I said. "And if there's one place where people need cheering up with a good cupcake, the hospital would be it."

"It might be too much work. I mean, would we have to bake every day?" she asked, already trying to schedule it in her mind.

"Maybe we could do it once a week?" Katie suggested.

"Yeah, and we could do specialty cupcakes for the hospital, too! Like the vampire ones could be for blood transfusions! Or we could do a jelly bean topping and call it the Tonsillectomy. Tonsils look like jelly beans, you know," said Mia, all fake serious.

"Not Jake's!" I said. "His were like golf balls, the doctor said."

"Eeeewww!" everyone said in unison, laughing but grossed out.

"Listen, guys, seriously about the vampire cupcakes. I think we need a warning on those or something."

Mia looked thoughtful. "Like a little sign to go on the platter?"

"Uh-huh."

"Eat at your own risk?" joked Katie.

"Exactly!" I said.

"Not a bad idea," agreed Alexis. "Better to be prepared . . ." She trailed off.

"Yeah, yeah." We all laughed. Alexis is all about preparation.

Mia inked out a little sign in neat handwriting on a white doily, then she attached it to a folded piece of white cardstock, so it would stand up. It said exactly what we'd wanted:

Vampire Cupcakes

Eat at your own risk!

(With a napkin under your chin!)

"Perfect!" I said. "Now, what kind of cupcakes would you make for a cute guy getting ankle surgery?" And then I told them all about my Diego encounter.

That night, my dad carried Jake down to the TV room where we all had a picnic dinner on a blanket on the floor. Jake had vanilla ice cream again; his throat hurt too much to subject it to any of the specialty ice creams my mom had let him stock up on last week. I could tell he felt lousy because he didn't even fight it. My dad ordered up an *Ice Age* movie that Jake requested, and we all watched it.

"Can we do this always?" Jake croaked a few minutes into the dinner and movie.

Sam tousled Jake's hair.

"Well, I don't know about always, sweetheart. It's not the *most* comfortable place to eat dinner . . . ," said my mom.

"But we can do it sometimes," agreed my dad.

"Fridays," said Jake, his eyes starting to droop.

"We'll see," said my mom.

My parents looked at each other as Jake began to fall asleep right there before our eyes. They smiled.

"Hey, can I take you up to bed?" asked Sam.

Jake nodded, his eyes still closed.

Sam gently scooped him off the floor and lifted him high onto his shoulder. Jake wrapped his arms across Sam's back and laid his head on Sam's shoulder, so he could continue to sleep. We all smiled at how cute it was, especially Sam.

"We'll be up in a minute to tuck you in, sweetheart," said my mom. "And we'll be taking turns to check on you all night."

They left the room, and we were all quiet for a moment, kind of watching *Ice Age*.

Then Matt said, "I like the new, tame Jake." We all nodded and laughed.

"Maybe they took out his temper when they took out his tonsils!" I said hopefully.

"I wish!" my mom groaned.

"We're very proud of you four kids," said my dad. "You're very good to one another."

"Most of the time," added my mom with a wink.

"And, Emma, you were terrific today. We couldn't have done it without you. Thanks, sweetheart," said my dad.

My mom nodded. "And I'm so proud of how brave you were. I know you were nervous in the lab room where you'd already fainted once this week. But you set a great example for Jake with your bravery."

"You're the best kind of sister a brother could have," agreed my dad.

"I'm the *only* sister he has!" I laughed.

My parents went up to check on Jake, and Matt and I were alone in the TV room.

"Was it gnarly?" he asked, not taking his eyes off the screen.

"Not too bad, really," I said. "I mean, I wasn't the one getting the operation, so I didn't see much."

"I'm kind of squeamish too," he admitted.

"Really? No way!" I couldn't believe that.

He looked at me. "Uh-huh. Like, one time, at

practice, Jamie Fernandez got hit with a ball right on his eyebrow, and it split open and you could, like, see the bone underneath, and the skin was kind of flapping on either side, and the blood was just pouring down his face, all in his eye. . . ."

And that's when I realized Matt was just teasing me. I couldn't believe I fell for it.

"I hate you!" I cried, slamming him with a throw pillow from the sofa.

He ducked, laughing. "Got ya!"

"Ugh! Brothers!" I yelled.

But later that night, as I tiptoed down the hall to my room, I heard Jake quietly calling my name.

"Jake?" I whispered.

"Come, Emmy," he said.

I went into his room.

"Will you and the girls make me my very own big bowl of frosting, like you promised?"

"Oh, sure, Jake. No problem." I couldn't believe he'd remembered that!

"Thanks. Do you know what?"

"What?"

"I want to be a doctor when I grow up."

"Wow, Jake! That's a great idea! I'd be so proud of you. It's a lot of work, learning how to become a doctor, but I bet you'd be really good at it. . . ."

"And you have to be my nurse," he added, and he rolled over sleepily.

Oh boy.

"Thanks, Jake. That would be . . . divine. Just divine," I said. And I crossed my fingers behind my back. Then I smiled. Maybe Katie was right after all. Little boys really were made of sugar and spice and everything nice. Most of the time.

Want another sweet cupcake?
Here's a sneak peek
of the sixteenth book in the

CUPCAKE ⊛ DIARIES

series:

Alexis
and the missing
ingredient

Want another sweet cupcake?

Here's a sneak peek

of the sixteenth book in the

CUPCAKE DIARIES

series

Alexis

and the missing

ingredient

The Best-Laid Plans

$\mathcal{M}$ost people would be thrilled to have off a couple of random days from school in the middle of the term, but me—not so much. I hate to lose momentum. I also dislike it when my schedule is disrupted. I know it sounds nuts, but I'm the kid who listens to the radio on snow days hoping they don't say my school's name.

So all this is why I was just a little bit bummed out that it was Teacher Development Week at my school, and we'd have off Thursday and Friday. I know, I know, it's crazy, but like I said, I'm a creature of habit and I like structure.

I also do not really like making social plans. I am happy to go to most things that other people plan, but thinking up activities and getting everyone on board isn't my favorite thing to do. Don't get me wrong; I love planning most everything else. I plan most of our budgets and projects, but something like what we're going to do on a Saturday afternoon . . . not so much. I leave that to my friends in the Cupcake Club: Emma, Mia, and Katie. In fact, I mostly just count on Emma, who has been my best friend since we were little. We like to do the same stuff, and I always include her if I want to do something, like go to the movies, and vice versa. Somehow it just always works out that there's something to do.

Mia, on the other hand, is great at coming up with fun ideas, like, "Hey, let's all go to the mall and get our nails painted neon" or "Let's go to the department store and try on one of every kind of accessory" or "Let's do a time capsule!" Katie, too, comes up with clever plans, like making a gingerbread mansion or building a haunted house for Emma's little brother and his friends. I do admit I had a fun plan, when I convinced us all to go to the pep rally parade and game in costumes—with boys!—but that was an exception since it came from my desperate need to spend time with my crush, Matt Taylor.

So now I'm faced with four empty days in a

row and no plans, and Emma has the nerve to be going away!

Sure, she gave me plenty of advance warning, but her saying she's going camping with her family and my realizing I need to dream up some plans were not that connected in my mind until the last minute. (For me, the last minute means the weekend before.)

Emma and I were lying on the floor in my room, watching cute animals on YouTube, and she was counting out the reasons on her fingers of why she was dreading camping.

"Bugs, cold, uncomfortable, no bathrooms, bad food . . ."

"No me!"

"Right! No you, only boys except my parents . . ." Emma has three brothers. That's a lot of brothers.

"Wait! When are you gone from?" I asked.

Emma sighed. "We leave Wednesday, right after school. In fact, *from* school, I think. And then we don't get back until Sunday morning!"

"OMG. Four nights. That is long. And meanwhile, I'll be—Wait! What will I be doing?" I'd suddenly realized I had ignored my number-one motto (Failing to plan is planning to fail.) and had not made one plan for the weekend. I sat upright in shock. "So, wait. Wednesday night, I'll . . . do homework. Thursday *day* I can . . . do a little more, like, extra-credit homework and tie up any loose Cupcake Club business. Maybe work on my speech for the Future Business Leaders of America Summit." I relaxed a little, realizing I could fill the days with getting ahead on my work. I took a deep breath. "But Thursday night, Friday? *Friday* night? Saturday and *Saturday night*? Oh no. That's a lot of time to fill!" I twirled my hair nervously. "What should I do?"

Emma looked at me. "You are so lucky. I'd kill to be doing nothing." She sighed.

"So stay! You can totally stay with me!" I started to relax again immediately, imagining the luxury of having a built-in best friend for four days. I grinned. "There's so much fun stuff we could do. I'm sure you'd have lots of great ideas!"

Emma sighed again heavily. "I can't. It's required. My mom thinks it might be our last camping trip as a family before Sam goes away to school."

My heart sank. "Hmph!" I said.

"Maybe you and Dylan could do something?" she asked helpfully. "Go somewhere?" She shrugged.

I scowled. "Going anywhere with Dylan is not exactly a laugh a minute," I said. Though my older sister can be nice sometimes, mostly she doesn't want me around and isn't afraid to show it or let me know it. "Even if she would do anything with me," I added.

"What about your grandparents?"

"Wow. Wait a minute! *That* is not a bad idea! Even for a night that might be fun. I'll ask my mom to ask them." My grandparents live about an hour away in a rambling old farmhouse that's filled with cool stuff, and they have lots of land and a trampoline and a barn and everything. That could be good. I felt a tiny bit better just thinking of it.

Emma thought again. "Maybe Dylan would take you to the city?" she suggested, then we both laughed. If Dylan was going to the city, it certainly wouldn't be with me. "Okay, okay. Just brainstorming."

"Hey! Speaking of brainstorming, we've got to resolve that PTA meeting menu."

"Oh boy." Emma closed her eyes and put her head in her hands.

We'd had one of our rare Cupcake Club blow ups the day before, just talking about what we should bake for the PTA meeting we were hired to cater in two weeks.

Our business, the Cupcake Club, bakes and sells

custom cupcakes for all kinds of events. Along with Mia and Katie, Emma and I have built a pretty good business of baking, with regular clients and signature recipes and great reviews on our website. PTA meetings and things like that are good venues for us, because there are lots of local parents all in one place, so we get to wow them with our skills and hopefully get new business out of some of them. It's a great way to earn some money and it's a ton of fun, too.

I am the business-minded brain of the group—the CEO. I plan our schedules, do the purchasing and manage the inventory, work out pricing—stuff like that. I realize it's funny that I am great at plans and schedules for work and for school, but terrible at it socially. It's just the way I am. My mom always says, you can't be great at everything, so be great at the most important things. That's what I try to do.

Anyway, during our meeting yesterday, all four of us had different ideas. Some of us wanted to go plain and basic, others wanted to really go wild and show what we were capable of. Two of us felt it was all about how great the cupcakes would look, while one said it was all about how they would taste, and the fourth member couldn't decide which was more important.

"All I know is, we need something really great because it's an ideal marketing opportunity for us. All those parents in one place . . . Those are our customers! Think of the birthday parties they organize, never mind book clubs and baby showers!" I said now to Emma.

Emma agreed. "I know, I know. I don't know why that turned into such a big fight. Mia and Katie were pretty upset."

"Well, they did seem better today, but that's probably because none of us brought it up."

Emma nodded. "We'll need to figure it out soon."

"A stitch in time saves nine," I agreed soberly.

Later, when Emma was leaving, she said, "Hey, don't forget Mia and Katie are around next weekend . . . at least for part of it. They'll have something fun going on for sure. Call them!"

"Right," I said. "Will do." But, in fact, I probably wouldn't. Even though I spend a lot of time with Mia and Katie, it's kind of like our foursome is a combination of two pairs: Mia and Katie are one, and Emma and I are the other. All together, the four of us are a great group, and two by two, we are good pairs. But I have never really hung out with just Mia or just Katie, and I don't really ever hang out with them without Emma. It's just the way it works out. I would almost be kind of nervous to hang out with them without Emma. I know it sounds nuts, but that's just how I feel. Anyway, I still had weird feelings about them since the PTA fight. I figured I'd be laying low for a while.

As soon as I shut the door after Emma, I called up to my mom, "Mom! Can you call Grandma to see if I can go stay with her this week?"

Then I ran to my desk and sent out an e-mail asking the Cupcakers to meet next Sunday to brainstorm some ideas for the PTA meeting. It was chicken of me to do it via e-mail and to put it off for another week, but whatever. At least it was being addressed. Phew.

Anyway, that's how it came to be Thursday morning and how I was putting my toothbrush into my already-packed overnight bag to go to my grandma's house. My granddad Jim was picking me up at nine, and I was really looking forward to my two nights at their house. (Jim is actually my stepgranddad, but he's the only one I've ever known.) Tonight we would have a feast and watch scary movies and eat popcorn and my grandma's caramel brownies. Tomorrow we're going to go on a long hike around the property and then to see the new kittens in the barn and lots of other fun stuff. My grandma is a great cook, and she isn't stingy with the butter or sugar the way my health-nut mom is. I knew I'd be eating well and sleeping well and getting lots of personal attention at the farmhouse, since Dylan was staying home so that she could go to the city with friends for the day. (She always has major plans, way in advance.) It was going to be great.

I heard the phone ring as I started down the stairs and kind of absentmindedly noticed it was a little early for the phone to ring. When I got to the kitchen, my mom was speaking urgently and had one hand gripping the countertop so hard, her knuckles were white.

My mom spoke anxiously into the phone. "Is she going to be okay? What did the doctor say it was?" She looked at me but didn't really register my presence. I dropped my bag to the floor. Who was she talking about?

"How long are they keeping her?"

Pause.

"Can we come out and help you?"

Dylan walked in and stood next to me, and we watched my mom talk on the phone.

Who? mouthed Dylan.

My mom stared blankly at us.

"Okay, well, please call me as soon as she comes back, and I can drive out there later this morning. Thanks so much, Jim. Give her a huge hug from us."

Dylan and I looked at each other in shock. Grandma?

Our mom hung up the phone and sat heavily at the kitchen table.

"Mom?" I asked quietly.

She looked up, and her eyes were teary. "It's fine. It just caught me off guard. Sorry. It's Grandma, but they think she's going to be okay. She fell down the stairs in the basement and bumped her head, so they took her to the hospital to make sure she was okay."

"Oh!" My hand flew to my mouth.

My mom smiled. "Well, you know Grandma can be a little clumsy. Jim said it could have been a lot worse, and she's in very good hands. They really think she's going to be fine. They're keeping her at the hospital for observation, just to be safe. She'll just need to rest and take it easy for a few days."

"That's scary, Mom," said Dylan, reaching over to rub my mom's back. I wished I'd thought of that.

"Poor Grandma!" I said. "You're going to see her later?"

My mom nodded. "Jim said I didn't need to come, but I hate to think of him out there at the hospital all alone. I'll go into work for a bit this morning, then head straight out and probably spend the night at the house. And you girls can—Oh, Lexi! I just realized! It was your special trip today. I'm so sorry, honey!" She got up to give me a hug.

"That's okay," I said into her shoulder. "Do you want me to come with you to the hospital, anyway?"

She let go and smoothed back my hair. "No, but thank you. I think I'd better go alone. Maybe Dad could take you girls out for a treat tonight, since you're missing your trip, Lexi."

I nodded. "Okay. And maybe we could watch a movie."

"Sure," she said. She picked up her cell phone to look at her day's schedule and then she called my dad to tell him the new plan.

Dylan and I looked at each other. "Well . . . ," she said.

"I'm going to just do my homework today," I said. I could see her relief.

"Okay, are you sure?" Dylan asked.

"Totally," I said. Nobody wants to go where they're not welcome.

"Okay."

And that was that.

Mirror, Mirror

Here's where Emma does her hair and makeup. Look at this picture for thirty seconds, then turn the page.
Can you find the six differences in the second picture?
Circle each one you find.

Can you find the six differences on this page from the
page before? Circle each one you find.

(If you don't want to write in your book, make a copy of this page.)

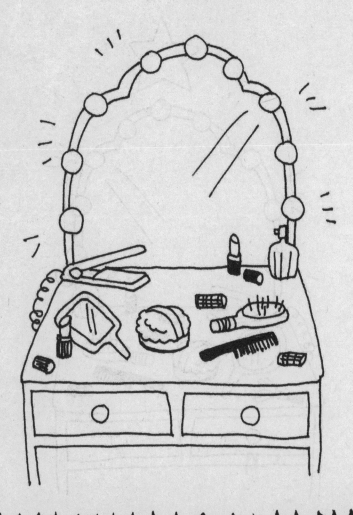

Puzzle It Out

All the words below are words you've just read in Emma Sugar and Spice and Everything Nice. But they are all scrambled. Unscramble each word and write it correctly on the lines. Then take the letters that appear in the circles, and write them in order on the lines below. You'll find out something that happens in the next Cupcake Diaries book, Alexis and the Missing Ingredient.

(If you don't want to write in your book, make a copy of this page.)

KIGNAB   B(a)king

STORFGNI   fr o s t i(n)g

ROOTARCNS   _(_)_ _ _ _ _ _

SHRUC   _(_)_ _ _

LUGARRE   _ _(_)_ _ _ _

SIBUNESS   _(_)_ _ _ _ _ _

DELMO   (_)_ _ _ _

DEVOI   _ _ _(_)_

ESION   (_)_ _ _ _

TALPIOHS   _ _ _ _ _(_)_ _

In *Alexis and the Missing Ingredient*, Mia and Katie get into a n _ _ _ _ _ _ _ _ _ _ _.

ANSWER KEY

Mirror, Mirror

Puzzle It Out

KIGNAB	B A K I N G
STORFGNI	F R O S T I N G
ROOTARCNS	C A R T O O N S
SHRUC	C R U S H
RALUGER	R E G U L A R
SIBUNESS	B U S I N E S S
DELMO	M O D E L
DEVOI	V I D E O
ESION	N O I S E
TALPIOHS	H O S P I T A L

In *Alexis and the Missing Ingredient,* Mia and Katie get into
<u>A N   A R G U M E N T.</u>

Coco Simon always dreamed of opening a cupcake bakery but was afraid she would eat all of the profits. When she's not daydreaming about cupcakes, Coco edits children's books and has written close to one hundred books for children, tweens, and young adults, which is a lot less than the number of cupcakes she's eaten. Cupcake Diaries is the first time Coco has mixed her love of cupcakes with writing.

Want more

CUPCAKE DIARIES?

Visit **CupcakeDiariesBooks.com**
for the series trailer, excerpts, activities,
and everything you need for throwing
your own cupcake party!

Simon
Spotlight

Still Hungry?

There's always room for another Cupcake!

Katie and the Cupcake Cure

Mia in the Mix

Emma on Thin Icing

Alexis and the Perfect Recipe

Katie, Batter Up!

Mia's Baker's Dozen

Emma All Stirred Up!

Alexis Cool as a Cupcake

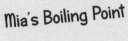

Looking for another great book?
Find it in the middle.

in
the
middle
BOOKS

Fun, fantastic books for kids
in the in-beTWEEN age.

IntheMiddleBooks.com

SIMON & SCHUSTER
Children's Publishing   f /SimonKids

If you liked

CUPCAKE DIARIES

be sure to check out these

other series from

Simon Spotlight

31901064881289